Assaulted Souls II

by

I0552214

William Blackwell

This book is a work of fiction. Names, characters, places and incidents are either the product of the author's imagination or are used fictitiously. Any resemblance to actual persons, living or dead, or to actual events or locales is entirely coincidental.

Assaulted Souls II

Copyright © 2016 WILLIAM BLACKWELL PUBLISHING. All rights reserved, including the right to reproduce this book, or portions thereof, in any form. With the exception of brief quotes used for review purposes, no part of this text may be reproduced, transmitted, downloaded, decompiled, reverse engineered, or stored in or introduced into any information storage and retrieval system, in any form or by any means, whether electronic or mechanical, without the express written permission of the publisher.

Cover designed by Telemachus Press, LLC

Published by Telemachus Press, LLC

ISBN: 978-1-7389714-8-0 (paperback)

Version: 2016.12.10

Acknowledgements

Heartfelt thanks to my loyal and supportive readers, friends and family, the hardworking staff at Telemachus Press, and my editor. Special thanks to the Government of Prince Edward Island for its financial support.

The world breaks everyone and afterward many are strong in the broken places. But those that will not break it kills. It kills the very good and the very gentle and the very brave impartially. If you are none of these you can be sure it will kill you too but there will be no special hurry.

–Ernest Hemingway, *A Farewell to Arms*

Hell is empty and all the devils are here.
    –William Shakespeare

Assaulted Souls II

Prologue

"That's how it is."

"What's that supposed to mean?"

"Your death."

"I'm not dead."

"But you will be. We all will be. We won't live forever, you know."

"But I'm too young to die. I'm afraid to die."

"It's part of the journey. Be at peace with it. Embrace it."

"Are you telling me I'm going to die?"

"Yes, you're going to die."

"When?"

"Very soon."

"How? How am I going to die?"

"Painfully."

"Is that all you can say? 'Painfully?' Tell me more."

"In time, young son. In time. Not everything at once. You're too afraid right now. You need to find the courage to face it."

"This conversation is getting old real fast. Who the fuck are you? Why don't you tell me when and how I'm going to die? Maybe you don't know shit. Have you ever thought about that? Maybe you're not even real and this is some fucked up nightmare? You won't tell me because it isn't true. You're not real. This is a nightmare. I'm alive and well and living ..."

"Living, yes, where are you living? Rescued from a post-apocalyptic wasteland. Now you're in the hands of the government. What do you think they're doing to you?"

"Killing me?"

"As I said, not all at once. You're not ready."

"Who are you?"

"I told you, not everything at once."

"Tell me who the fuck you are?"

"I'm sorry."

"Tell me."

"I'm sorry."

"Tell me when and how I'll die."

"That's not going to happen. But it's important you know one thing."

"What's that?"

"It's not so important that you're going to die. We're all slowly dying. What's important is how you live your life."

"That's a fucking corny and overused cliché if I ever heard one ... how am I supposed to live my life?"

"If you need to ask, you don't need to know."

Chapter One

Swimming up into consciousness, Nathan King thought for a terrifying moment he *was* dead. His heart pounded furiously in his chest and his white t-shirt was drenched in sweat. His eyes darted furtively around the room, looking for something recognizable, some tangible inanimate object to pin reality onto. Whitewashed sterile walls were all he saw. It wasn't convincing. He gasped, trying to steady his breathing, and pinched his hand. The stinging pain was real enough to remind him of his situation. He lay there for a few seconds, staring at the ceiling and waiting for his heart rate to steady, not wanting to think about it until he felt stable enough to do so.

A nightmare, he thought, a moment later. *The third time I've had that nightmare. What does it mean?* The conversation with the unidentified man in the nightmare never failed to lend scary significance to his current situation. He always struggled to interpret it, only to dismiss it a few minutes later.

The scene was always the same. A gray, barren landscape; a post-apocalyptic crimson sky; the ominously glowing red eyes; the body-less voice; the conversation. And he still didn't recognize the person behind the voice. Was it Edward Sole, the man who had heroically died fighting off the marauding Neanderthals while he, Cadence Whittaker, and Velvet Jones escaped? Was it Edward Sole, the man who had gone stark-raving mad just prior to their escape and almost murdered them?

"If you need to ask, you don't need to know," Nathan thought, recollecting snippets of the conversation. *Is that Ed, telling me*

to find purpose in my life because he failed at that? And I'm going to die. Very soon. And painfully. The government. What do you think they're doing to you? What the fuck is going on? Forget it. It's a dream, nothing more. You've just been through a shit-storm. Your girlfriend was just murdered. You're in shock. You're healing. You'll get over it. Forget it. That's how it is.

But why did it feel so real? And what did it mean? And why wouldn't anyone give him a straight answer? His queries in quarantine had been met with answers such as "in due time ... wait until you recover and we'll tell you everything ... you're in shock ... it'll all come out in the wash ... you'll love your new home." He sat up in bed, wiped his glistening forehead, and surveyed the utilitarian-furnished white padded room

He didn't know how long he had been quarantined. Commander Randall Stiessman and military Doctor Stan Imes had said a month was all it would take after the dramatic chopper rescue from the infected nuclear holocaust zone. But it felt like he had been in that prison-like room a lot longer. After a week in a sterilized, heavily guarded and tightly sealed infirmary, he had been transferred to the quarantine wing of the large military aircraft carrier floating in the Atlantic Ocean somewhere off the coast of Newfoundland, The Rock.

First imprisoned in a dark cave in a nightmarish existence with mutant animals, opportunistic murdering savages, the decaying sanity of allies, the struggle for survival, food, sanity and safety. Only to survive to be quarantined in a white padded room with a bathroom, a few sticks of furniture, fuzzy television screen, three meals a day passed through hermetically-sealed chambers, little or no contact with humans and no questions answered.

He had been inches away from losing his sanity in the end-of-days horrifying struggle on Prince Edward Island and The Rock. Now, floating on a ship, essentially cut off from all human contact, he felt a couple of inches away from losing his grip on reality. *I'm in a padded room. Where the fuck is the straitjacket? Floating on a boat? Isn't that how I almost died last time? Floating on a fishing boat?*

He climbed out of bed, scowled at the motion-sensitive video camera whirring and watching, walked into the bathroom, and examined his face in the mirror. His green eyes were clear, but the dark circles remained. His once long brown hair had been trimmed into a crew cut. He sported three-day facial stubble. His once full cheeks were still gaunt, the result of malnourishment, scavenging for food in a world with no amenities, where money didn't amount to jack shit.

Nathan saw sadness in his eyes. A sadness that had not disappeared since Cadence Whittaker, his girlfriend, was shot in the head by Karl Mulligan, the then-leader of the ruthless Neanderthal gang that had terrorized PEI post-apocalypse. He still harbored guilt about letting her venture into the barn that fateful day with their friend Velvet Jones. After all, what were they really there for? Some sticks of dynamite and a photo of Velvet's daughter, Lisa? *Sentimental bullshit that cost Cadence her life.*

Nathan tried a smile that emerged as more of a wince. He didn't know if he'd ever get over the guilt, the mourning for Cadence. It helped, he thought, that Karl Mulligan had paid for his crime with a crushed skull, compliments of Nathan delivering repeated rage-filled blows to the psycho's head with a baseball bat.

It helped a little.

But not a lot.

He sighed, pulling off his t-shirt and examining his ribs. They still poked through skin. But he had put on a few pounds after arriving on the ship. He was far from the shadow of a man he had been trying to survive in that cold, dank and smelly network of caves a short time ago. Then, he was as skinny and frail as a twig, like a man stricken with a terminal disease with only a few short weeks to live.

Feeling like a laboratory rat, he showered quickly, dressed in white boxer briefs, white cotton pants, white t-shirt, white socks and slippers. He emerged into the white living room just as the buzzer sounded on a remote control on a white coffee table beside a white couch. He sat on the couch, picked up the remote and pressed a button. A built-in wall-screen illuminated and the face of Doctor Stan Imes transformed from cloudy to clear. Imes, dressed in a white smock with black-framed nerd glasses, grinned. He had a habit of running a hand through his curly black mid-length afro. He held a computer tablet in his hands, studying something on the screen. He looked up.

"Nathan, how are you this morning?"

"When are you letting me out of here?" The doctor would visit every other day, occasionally take blood samples, check vitals, dispense so-called anti-radiation injections and inquire about Nathan's health. Imes had lots of questions but very few answers. For example, Nathan was quarantined, but nobody who came near him wore hazmat suits, rubber gloves or respirators of any kind. Since he'd arrived on the ship, not a lot made any sense. The good doctor was evasive when Nathan inquired about the communicability of the virus.

"I'm outside your door," Imes said. "Can I come in?"

"You have remote access. I can't stop you."

"I'm trying to respect your privacy. I have some good news for you."

Nathan waved at the screen and clicked the off button on the remote. It faded to black. Imes entered and sat in a chair facing Nathan. "You're almost done with your quarantine."

"How long do I have left?"

"We're releasing you tomorrow."

Nathan sighed. Finally. "How long have I been here?"

"One month less a day."

"You haven't told me that before."

"Oh, but I have. We discussed it a few days ago. It must be your amnesia. You're still not a hundred per cent."

"What amnesia?"

"You don't remember?"

"No."

"You had a fall in PEI prior to detonation."

Nathan scratched his head while Imes ran a hand through his afro. Maybe they were answering his questions and he just couldn't remember? *Note to self: Self, don't be too aggressive with these people.* "Oh, right. It's coming back to me."

"You remember?"

"Bits and pieces."

"It seems the fall injured your brain more than we thought," Imes said, studying his tablet. His brow wrinkled. "But let's move on, shall we?"

"Okay."

"All of our tests to this point show you haven't contracted the virus. It seems you're immune, but you can understand that we had to be sure. You were obviously exposed to radiation, but our tests show the levels to be below the danger point. It seems you'll be able to live a happy and healthy life."

"Happy and healthy life? In this wasteland?"

"We're going to relocate you."

"Where?"

"It's a man-made experimental island about a hundred miles from here. We call it District 101. Commander Stiessman will fill you in tomorrow."

"He's coming to see me?"

"Yes."

"What can you tell me about District 101?"

"Commander Stiessman will fill you in. But I think you'll like it. It's unlike anything else technology has ever produced." Imes paused for a moment. "I have some more good news."

"You're just a bundle of joy today."

"It would be nice if you could refrain from sarcasm."

"I'm serious."

"You remember Velvet Jones?"

"Yeah." That much he did remember. Velvet was instrumental in his escape from the wasteland. It was also her idea to retrieve ammunition and a photo from her property prior to leaving—an idea that cost Cadence her life. Nathan's memory of Velvet was bittersweet. Bitter, because he still held her partly responsible for Cadence's death. Sweet, because after Cadence's murder, Nathan and Velvet had had a hell of a fuck session. It had been so satisfying, Nathan still dreamed about the carnal encounter, reconstructing surreal and erotic variations of it in his subconscious. That was something he didn't think he could ever erase from his damaged memory.

"You want to visit with her tonight?" Imes asked.

Nathan craved conversation and contact with someone almost more than anything right now, even though he had mixed emotions about Velvet. "Are you letting me out to see her?"

"We'll bring Velvet to you. You can order anything you want on the menu. We'll even bring in some candles and a wine list."

"That would be great." *Really, how great? Stranded in the middle of the ocean, quarantined on this ship, about to be transported to a new life on an experimental island, about to meet the one woman who reminds me more than anything of Cadence, my only soulmate who is now a pile of bones and ashes somewhere on Prince Edward Island. Shut up. Get over it already. A new world. A new start. Healthy and happy.*

Chapter Two

"We want you to be healthy and happy," Doctor Imes said a few hours later, approaching Velvet with a syringe. "So you need your injection."

"Well I don't want it anymore," Velvet said, furrowing a brow and brushing a lock of long black hair away from her eyes. "I told you I'm fine. That shit makes me dizzy."

"You need it."

"What do I need it for?"

"I told you before."

"Well, tell me again."

"Pamerexol-744 is an anti-radiation drug designed to first contain the radiation in your body, then collect it and draw it to an area away from your vital organs where the drug eventually attacks and destroys it."

"Well it must have worked, because I feel fine."

"Our tests show you still need a few more treatments."

"My internal health meter tells me that isn't so."

Imes took a step closer to Velvet, who sat on the bed, eying him cautiously. He raised the syringe and extracted some rubber tubing from a black medicine bag. "Now roll up your sleeve and let's get this over with."

Velvet stood. "If you value that hand, don't take another step forward."

It hadn't been the first time she had displayed insolence. Two previous altercations with medical and military staff had resulted in heavy sedation, strong arms and a straitjacket. It had only been a week since she had removed the straitjacket from her closet and crossed it off the preferred-list-of-fashion-conscious-clothes-to-wear.

Corporal Rice Sterling, armed with an AK-47 machine gun, wearing camouflaged military fatigues and polished black leather boots, stepped from his post. "I don't think you can handle this, Imes."

Imes waved him away. "I can handle this."

Sterling took two steps back, resuming his guard position at the door. But he didn't take his eyes off Imes. And it wasn't a friendly come-for-tea kind of look.

"Do you think you can handle me?" Velvet said, clenching her fists. "Or have you already forgotten that black eye I gave you last time?"

Imes stepped back, lowering the syringe. "Let me ask you a question. Since we've started anti-radiation therapy, do you feel better now than you did a month ago? You remember how lethargic you were when we first got here?"

"I suppose surviving a post-apocalyptic wasteland with ruthless killers, murderous zombies and attacking mutant animals might make a person a little lethargic afterward."

"I'm not talking about that. Don't you feel more energetic and focused since we've started treatments?" He pointed to her arms. "And the radiation rash. It's all but gone."

Velvet's battle-hardened features returned to something approximating normal. She rolled up her sleeve and glanced at her right arm. It was true. The red and black spots had faded noticeably. And they no longer itched, burned and throbbed with pain. Maybe Imes was telling the truth? Maybe they weren't using her as a guinea pig for some personality-altering medication that would allow them to control her? After all, she still had the violent Velvet edge—the edge that kept her sane and kept her breathing. That hadn't disappeared. But the rash. The rash was healing nicely. And she had felt her former energy starting to return, even be replaced with some force far more restless and itching for rigorous physical activity. Her progress on the exercise bike of late had been nothing short of remarkable. Furiously-paced one-hour sessions had given way to two, then three, and now she was up to four hours of non-stop fifty-mile-an-hour sessions while barely breaking a sweat. She was getting stronger. That had to be a good thing. Didn't it?

"The rash is almost gone," she said.

"And your energy?"

"I feel better ... but after the injection, I feel dizzy."

"That will pass. It's the radiation attacking your body, attacking P-744. Look at it this way. Your body's immune system is forming an alliance with the drug. The radiation is trying to break up the alliance. Once radiation senses an invasion, it moves to attack it. But the drug teams up with your body's immune system to destroy the radiation. I'm sure you can attest to the fact the dizzy feeling doesn't last long."

"About an hour."

"That's because it takes all your body's strength to fight off a fresh attack from the radiation. But it goes away and you feel better than ever. Am I right?"

"I suppose."

"And, correct me if I'm wrong, but hasn't the duration of the dizzy spells shortened? How long were you dizzy when we first started this?"

"Maybe three hours. And sometimes the dizziness would make me sick to my stomach."

"But, not anymore. Am I right?"

"It's true."

"And look at the progress you're making with your exercise. No one can argue with that."

Velvet sighed, sat down on the bed and rolled up her right sleeve. "Get it over with. How many more injections will I need?"

Imes sat, tied a rubber tube around her bicep, tapped her arm a few times, extracted an alcohol swab, wiped a bulging vein clean and inserted the syringe. "Just a little pinch. There. I think another four or five and you'll be as good as gold."

He reached into his medical bag and extracted a cotton swab and some medical tape. He finished the injection, removed the syringe, and applied the cotton baton with tape to the small wound. "All set, Velvet."

Velvet's eyes swam in her head. The room spun. She slid up to the pillow and rested her head on it.

He stood up, packing away the instruments. "That's it. Just lie down and relax. The dizziness will pass and you'll feel better than ever. Remember, you have a date with Nathan tonight—your first date in a month."

"Leave me in peace," Velvet said, the wave of dizziness pushing her eyelids closed. "I feel like a caged rat."

After Imes and Sterling had left, she couldn't help smelling a rat. Something wasn't right. She was skeptical of District 101. Too many unanswered questions, not least of which was what kind of freedom would she have in a glass-domed, atmosphere and temperature-controlled environment, trying to forge a harmonious existence with other post-apocalyptic survivors? There would probably be surveillance and video cameras everywhere. Hell, for all she knew the Canadian military had already installed a tracking microchip in her head. Control with the illusion of freedom. Sounds like something the government would do—and had already done.

But Velvet was sure of one thing. She would do everything in her power to resist this control, to assert her personal liberties and freedoms. And if Imes and Commander Stiessman didn't release her when they promised, there would be hell to pay. She slid her hand underneath her pillow slowly, conscious of the closed-circuit TV monitors watching her every move. She felt the cold steel of the military-issue combat knife and smiled. She had nicked it from Sterling three days ago while tempting him with a kiss, just outside video-camera range. She had withdrawn at the last second, expertly unsheathed the combat knife, and now the weapon was her bedmate and protector—her personal knife in shining armor.

She had initially been surprised Sterling hadn't discovered the loss immediately and ordered a complete search of her room. But as the days passed without a search, she realized it wasn't Sterling's style. He was in line for a promotion and the last thing he would do was admit the loss of a weapon to a patient, or inmate. One step forward. Three steps back.

Velvet slowly felt sleep sapping conscious thought. On one hand, she wanted to fight it, but on the other she wanted to return to the recurring nightmares of fierce battles in the bomb-devastated, savage-infested wasteland that was once pretty Prince Edward Island. At least there the rules were simple—kill or be killed. She knew where she stood, knew how to survive, knew how to kill. But now, imprisoned, injected, prodded, poked and watched 24/7, that fierce warrior metaphorically sat cross-legged in the middle of a bloody and corpse-filled battlefield, meekly waving a white flag.

Not for long, Velvet thought. *Not for long.*

As her finger gently caressed the spine of the blade underneath her pillow, she allowed conscious thought to evaporate and welcomed the nightmarish images forming in her subconscious as a blanket of sleep enveloped her.

******

She was crouched behind a rock outcrop, the crimson sun setting in the distance casting an orange haze on a black and bleak debris-and-dead-body strewn battlefield. She fired the machine gun at attacking, frothing, rage-filled mutant zombies.

Rat-a-tat-tat ... rat-a-tat-tat ... rat-a-tat-tat!

Rat in a cage ... rat in a cage ... rat in a cage.

Rat-a-tat-tat ... rat-a-tat-tat ... rat-a-tat-tat!

Rat in a cage ... rat in a cage ... rat in a cage.

For a moment, silence.

Then the maddening moaning sound echoing eerily from a half dead man sprawled on top of a pile of bodies nearby. Then the steady grating sound—purposeful footfalls scraping along the ground—as incoming zombies beat a path to her rock-outcrop doorstep.

Realizing the machine gun magazine was spent, Velvet popped it out, reached for another clip, and slammed it into place. It found a home with a metallic click.

The half dead man, puss oozing from large scabby blisters covering his face, spoke between moans. "Kill me ... kill me please."

Velvet swung the machine gun over her shoulder, stood up and moved toward him. His chest was riddled with a V of blood-oozing bullet holes—a Velvet signature since becoming proficient with the machine gun.

But wait. Something's wrong. Zombies don't speak. They kill, growl, snarl and stagger around aimlessly. But speak? Never. Shit. I killed an innocent. Collateral damage. Fuck it.

Velvet bent down on one knee and stared into the dying man's brown eyes. In those eyes she saw resignation, acceptance, and relief. This man, whoever he was, was thankful that the terrifying struggle was almost over. A wave of compassion swept over her. Tight facial features softened. "Did you say something?"

The man opened his mouth to speak, while pointing to her sheathed combat knife. Blood dribbled down his cheek. "Kill ... kkkill ... me."

She turned to the battlefield. The zombies were now within twenty feet and scraping closer. There was no time for talk, no time for eulogies, no time for apologies. Life was simple again, distilled to its base essence—kill or be killed.

She pointed the machine gun at the zombies.

Rat-a-tat-tat ... rat-a-tat-tat ... rat-a-tat-tat!

Zombies dropped to the ground, moaning while they died, some adorned with the signature V. Then silence again. She had a few minutes before the next wave of mindless murderers would arrive.

She unsheathed her combat knife, turned to the dying man. "Any last words?"

"They put me here."

"Who ... who put you here?"

"Kill me ... please."

Fuck it. He's out of his mind. She plunged the knife deep into his throat. He gasped as rivulets of blood spurted from his mouth and fatal neck wound. Then he was still—intense, assaulted, soulful eyes boring into Velvet.

Like an icepick, a thought pierced the floor of her subconscious ... "*They put me here.*"

"*Who ... who put you here?*"

Chapter Three

"I put you here to do a job," Commander Randall Stiessman snapped. "Now do it."

Doctor Imes wore an embarrassed and humiliated expression—like a young child who has just been scolded for wetting the bed—as he stared down at his computer tablet for answers. He sat across from Stiessman at a boardroom table in one of many control rooms in the well-equipped and high-tech floating city. Computer and radar screens—occupying two walls—beeped intermittently. Fans hummed and colorful geometric patterns danced across screens. A digital world map occupied another wall, luminescent yellow dots marking a dozen locations. Yet another wall had built-in monitors displaying real-time images of various locations on the ship, including two screens that tracked and recorded Velvet and Nathan's every sleeping and waking moment. Imes felt his face flush. "I'm doing my job, sir. I thought P-744 would work quicker, that's all."

"Once you could see it wasn't working fast enough, why didn't you increase the dosage?" Stiessman asked. He had hard, intense black eyes, sharp facial features, a thick black handlebar mustache, and bushy eyebrows a centimeter apart from forming a unibrow. His black hair was cropped in a crew cut, his uniformed chest glittering with medals of bravery and authority. Fastidious and efficient with detail, the commander ran a tight ship—everything in its place and a place for everything. He had little patience for deviation from his ordered life and plans. He had higher-ups to answer to and hadn't gotten this far by tolerating inefficiency. His eyes bored into Imes and a tiny vein snaked its way across his neck, pulsating and growing.

Imes finally looked up from his tablet, immediately averting his eyes from the commander's penetrating stare, preferring instead to watch the vein's upward momentum and increasing girth. He finally spoke. "I was afraid, sir—maybe concerned is a better word. This drug is fresh out of experimental trials and ... well, as you know we've had some rather nasty side effects. Those side effects manifested themselves when we increased dosages without thinking through the ramifications. Now we know the ramifications. So we need to go slow and steady. Maybe it takes a little longer, but I believe it's better to err on the side of caution."

Stiessman bristled. "I don't have a little longer, Doctor Imes. Tomorrow night I have to answer to the prime minister of Canada and the president of the United States. Tell me, do you think they give a shit about erring on the side of caution?"

Imes knew it was a rhetorical question so didn't bother answering. But the word caution had evoked the painful memory of the first unfortunate P-744 test subject. Rescued from PEI a few weeks after the bomb blast, Melvin Tierney had no idea his terror was just beginning. He had been given the usual spiel by Doctor Imes during his quarantine on the ship. "We have to exercise caution. The government has your health and happiness foremost on its mind. This anti-radiation drug will kill the radiation in your body and prevent any life-threatening mutations or other life-threatening consequences. Please, take it. You'll be glad you did."

The young man had promptly rolled up his sleeve and acquiesced to the injection. Three injections later, he was the most loving, orderly, obedient man on the ship. He was even starting to hug Imes after each treatment, complimenting him on his good looks and bedside manner.

Exactly what the government wanted. Ordered, loving, law-abiding citizens who—after hearing the utterance of a secret number-letter combination—would instantly morph into ruthless, conscienceless but obedient killing machines. The enemy wouldn't stand a chance. Civilization would become peaceful and ordered—the entire population ready to take up arms in the country's defense at the mention of one code word. Military spending would drop, other countries would develop a healthy respect for the power of Canada and the United States, and terrorism and war would cease to exist. And another number-letter combination—delivered verbally or visually—would instantly stop the controlled aggression. As simple as turning off a kitchen tap. The citizens would have no idea what had possessed them to defend their country. But they would be glad they did. A new and loyal patriotism would be born, a love for the country and its people, a bond and kinship stronger than anything ever before seen in the human race—the dawn of a new era for humankind.

That was the theory.

The reality was something quite different. Imes noticed an unusual sexual nature to Melvin's loving, kind side. He often saw Melvin staring at his butt. One day Imes asked him if he was gay. Melvin had looked bewildered for a second, then grinned. "I like the pussy. And if you can find me some, doc—I've been hornier than a house-cat in heat lately—I'd be forever in your debt."

As it turned out, they had another female test subject, Larynda Roulson, dying to get laid. Imes thought he was doing them a favor putting them together for a nice dinner and a bottle of wine. Besides, he was curious how their lovemaking session would go. He could have a drink himself and watch the action on video—live streaming porn.

It had started off entertaining enough. They had eaten dinner, drank some wine, engaged in some casual, light-hearted conversation. Then Larynda stripped off her white jumper and wasted no time peeling off her black lace bra and panties. Imes still remembered growing erect staring at the screen, watching her tight ass, flat stomach, and pear-shaped, gravity-defying breasts with erect nipples jutting out as she danced around naked, grinning a come-fuck-me-now grin.

He had watched in enjoyment as Melvin and Larynda—test subjects zero-one and zero-two respectively—fucked and sucked each other in multiple positions on that small white bed. But that enjoyment was quickly replaced by a concerned frown. They were finishing up when Larynda pulled Melvin back on the bed and said: "Fuck me four times. I want number four."

The change in Melvin was as instantaneous as turning on a hot water tap. His boyish features had darkened. His face tensed and he said two words before attacking: "Fuck you."

Then he leaped on the bed, gouged out Larynda's eyes to horrific screams and tossed them against the wall. Next, he pummeled her repeatedly in the face. By the time guards had arrived, her face was a bleeding, disfigured mess of mangled blood, skull, guts and gray matter.

No guts and glory here.

Fucked to death? Imes thought. *Not quite. Fucked and savagely beaten to death.* It was a few days later, while examining the data, that Imes realized what had gone wrong. The number four was a number that was part of the aggression-inducing catalyst passcode. Even though there were other letters and numbers, the mere mention of the number four had triggered Melvin's violent impulses. And they were anything but controlled impulses, Imes thought, making a mental note to check in on Melvin later. With no recollection of what had happened, Melvin was locked away in a dungeon-like room deep in the bowels of the ship, awaiting reparative treatment.

"Are you hearing me, Doctor Imes?" Stiessman asked again. "The people I answer to couldn't care less about caution."

Caution. What caution? Imes pushed the painful memory deep into a walled compartment of his mind and addressed the commander. "With all due respect, sir, the last thing we want is the populace—what's left of it anyway—turning on each other, or turning on us. The whole idea of this drug is to create a peaceful existence."

"I thought you had that all worked out?"

"I do ... thought I did."

"Don't think, Doctor Imes. Do. Show me some results tonight." Stiessman examined the monitors showing Velvet and Nathan—test subjects zero-seven and zero-eight—in their respective rooms. Nathan sat on a couch, staring at white fuzz on a video screen, while Velvet slept, occasionally tossing and turning. "Do you think you can induce them to fuck and turn it off again without causing bodily harm?"

I think so. Don't think, do. "Yes sir."

"Do me a favor," Stiessman said, still examining the screen. "Up the dosage, just to be sure."

"Up the dosage?"

"Am I not speaking English? Up the fucking dosage."

"I have a small window to work with within the confines of what, in my professional opinion, would be a manageable increase."

"Well then work within that window. What do you think we're paying you for?"

The last sentence was delivered with a note of finality. The meeting was over.

Imes left, leaving Stiessman alone to examine papers and screens and determine the fate of what was left of humankind. All the power, all the control, all in the hands of one man. Imes knew only too well that Stiessman knew how to play US President Reese Stintson and Canadian Prime Minister Eliot Masterson like a seasoned conductor of a familiar orchestra.

What he didn't know was whether Velvet and Nathan's date tonight would turn into a macabre, deadly bloodbath.

Chapter Four

"I don't need a bath," Melvin Tierney said. "And my name's not Melvin. It's Melting Pot."

Doctor Imes felt goose bumps crawl up his arms as he stepped into the gray steel room. Since murdering Larynda, Melvin's loose grip on sanity had been gradually unravelling. Further treatments with P-744 had netted no positive results. If anything, the drug was causing Melvin to become more unstable and unpredictable. This wasn't the first time Imes had heard him rant and rave nonsense. What Melvin didn't know was that Commander Stiessman had given Imes one week to correct Melvin's worsening behavior. If Imes couldn't rescue Melvin from the black abyss of insanity, Melvin would receive a lethal injection, be fitted with a pair of concrete galoshes and tossed overboard into the ocean, where his body would slowly decay and be ravaged by scum-sucking bottom feeders.

But, as Imes stared at the mess in front of him, he knew he didn't have an easy job ahead. Melvin was sprawled out on his back on the floor, his face, arms and hands covered in human feces. Evidently, before lying down, he had taken handfuls of the excrement and in capital letters painted *Melting Pot* on the prison wall. Now, grinning benevolently, he moved his arms up and down, making a feces angel on the concrete floor. Not something the good doctor was happy to see. "Okay, Melting Pot, if you like ... you need a bath."

"Do you like my angel?"

Imes turned around, punched some digits into an intercom, and ordered two orderlies to come in. Then he studied Melvin, who was dressed in shit-stained white boxer briefs. The twenty-four-year-old had shortly-cropped brown hair, soulful brown eyes, perfect teeth, soft boyish features and a lean physique. Too bad about the insanity part, Imes thought. In better days Melvin must have had a lot of women chasing him. "Melvin, there's a toilet in the room. Why didn't you use that?"

Melvin stopped moving his arms and looked up at the doctor, a flicker of recognition in his intense eyes. "You're right, doc. You're always right." He slowly got to his feet and sat on the single bed. "I should get myself cleaned up for Larynda. Tonight's the night right?"

Imes was momentarily stumped. He had not been able to bring himself to tell Melvin he was a murderer; or that Larynda was currently sitting at the bottom of the ocean, probably being fed on by scum-sucking bottom feeders. "I'm sorry, Melvin. Larynda's sick right now. Maybe when she recovers."

"Doc, I'm Melting Pot. I'm a Melting Pot. Do you know my father was Dutch, his father was German? My mother was English, her father Scottish. But I was born in Canada. That makes me Melting Pot ... but the angel is coming to rescue me." Melvin pointed to the crude wings shit-painted on the floor. "See that. It's a sign."

Steve Trimble and Richard Banks—orderlies in white smocks—entered the room, Richard holding neatly-folded white towels and wheeling a mop-containing bucket of soapy water on wheels. Steve held a syringe in one hand and a container with a rubber tube and disinfectant cotton swabs in the other.

Melvin had gotten to know them a little.

They both scrunched their noses and grimaced at the sight.

"Richard is going to clean this mess up and Steve is going to give you something to relax," Imes said. "Then they're going to get you cleaned up. Is that okay?" Melvin had yet to physically harm or threaten any off the staff, but Imes couldn't be too careful. He had just killed a woman.

Melvin nodded and looked at his arms and hands, then at the brown angel wings on the concrete floor. They were spotted yellow with corn kernels. His eyes widened in surprise. "What happened, doc? Did I do that?"

Steve wiped Melvin's arm with a towel, disinfected it with a cotton swab, tied it off, found a vein and administered an injection. Richard began mopping the feces.

Imes sighed. "I'm afraid so."

Melvin's tense muscles relaxed as the sedative took effect. "What's happening to me, doc? Something's happening to me. What is it?"

Steve grabbed Melvin's arm and led him to the door. Melvin continued staring at Imes. They reached the door and Steve opened it.

"You lost your mother, father and girlfriend in the bomb blast," Imes said. "You're suffering from post-traumatic stress disorder. Why don't we talk after you get yourself cleaned up? I have a new medication that might help." Imes offered a plastic smile. He had racked his brain for an answer to Melvin's government-induced psychosis. Three other medications had produced no positive change. He finally decided a regiment of lithium, a medication for schizophrenics, might work. It was worth a shot. He was running out of time.

His hands trembling, Melvin stared at Imes, wide-eyed. "I hope you can help me, doc. I'm scared. Really scared."

Chapter Five

Maybe he was scared. Nathan had good reason to be. Every day he felt a little weirder, a little less in control of his emotions. It seemed to be a sort of internal love-hate conflict. One day he loved the world, the next day he hated it—hated mankind for destroying it. And the future on District 101, where he would eventually end up, didn't sound all that promising. Not without all of his memory back, not without Cadence. He had no idea the loss of a soulmate could be this debilitating. He had never been this close to death before. And his parents were also killed in the blast; but he wasn't grieving over them. Why? Because he couldn't remember them. Some of the pieces to the puzzle had been added for him. Imes had been good enough to do that.

Nathan came from a lower class family in Surrey, British Columbia, a municipality, according to Imes, that "had a lot of crime and a lot of rednecks." He was an only child. His father Thomas drove a taxi and his mother Anna sold beauty products at female house gatherings, or hen parties, as Nathan liked to call them. There must have been some estrangement there, as Nathan couldn't even get a mental image of the pair. All he remembered were bits and pieces of a lonely, isolated upbringing. Imes had promised to locate a picture of his parents, so Nathan still held out hope that one day a complete memory of his mother and father would emerge. He knew the memory of the late Cadence Whittaker was as fresh as the lasagna in front of him. *Cadence, Cadence, oh Cadence.*

He looked across at Velvet Jones. They faced each other at a round table for two. It was covered with a red table cloth, a plastic red rose in a single tiny vase, wine bottle, half-full glasses of red wine, and half-eaten vegetable lasagna and salad on dinner plates. In a decorative glass candleholder, a single candle flickered, its yellow flame offering a warm glow to the otherwise sterile environment.

Should I say it? Should I? Here I am looking at the woman responsible for Cadence's death. He was about to blurt out something accusatory: *Why the fuck did you decide to return to the barn for the stupid picture?* Then he thought better of it and bit his tongue.

Now was not the time or place. Velvet looked edible. And Nathan was getting horny.

So instead, he asked: "Are you scared?"

She looked at him suspiciously, as if she knew what was going on in that fragmented mind of his, and could tell by his grim expression he still resented her for Cadence's death. But her answer was delivered evenly and without anger. Velvet was a master at concealing emotion. Her seductive smile gave away little, other than to suggest she, too, was getting aroused. "It's not an emotion I'm all that familiar with ... or maybe I've learned to conquer it. Concerned maybe. You?"

Nathan stared into her eyes as faint stirrings of carnal desire tickled his groin. "I'm at odds with how I feel. Sometimes I'm really happy we survived the nightmare. Other times—with all this uncertainty—I think I'd be better off dead. Scared? I guess. Sometimes."

They were quiet for a moment, listening to music from overhead built-in speakers. The Rolling Stone's *Angie* played:

Angie, Angie, when will those clouds all disappear?
Angie, Angie, where will it lead us from here?
With no loving in our souls and no money in our coats
You can't say we're satisfied
But Angie, Angie, you can't say we never tried

Velvet sipped wine and finally asked, "Do you feel all right? I mean, your health."

Nathan flashed his eyes at the audio-video cameras listening and watching, and Velvet gave him a knowing look. "I feel fine. I'm getting stronger. But my memory isn't that good yet. You?"

"I'm stronger than ever. Kicking ass on the exercise bike and hardly breaking a sweat." Velvet talked about the fitness goals she had set and how she had exceeded them at every turn; how her body felt more toned than ever, her energy level increasing rapidly by the day.

While she talked, Nathan noticed a subtle, pleasing numbness wash over him—it was no longer faint. He looked at his half-full glass and wondered if it was just the wine. But no, there was something else—a powerful urge to grab Velvet roughly, force her onto the bed and have his way with her. The peek-a-boo cleavage view she sported in her low-cut V-neck blouse looked more attractive than ever. His mind drifted back to the time they had made love in that small two-story house in Newfoundland just before being over-run by zombies and separated by violent circumstance. He felt the tent rising in his blue jeans (for the occasion, they had been fitted with new clothes) and couldn't help the thoughts tumbling in his mind. *I want to suck her tits ... fuck her tits ... give it to her up the ass*

... fuck her pussy ... have her blow me ... oh-oh-oh ... how sweet it would be ...

Then Nathan realized she had stopped talking. He took a quick swallow of wine and met her gaze.

She winked. "Would you like to dance?"

He stood up. "Don't mind if I do."

They stepped away from the table and moved closer. Nathan put one hand on Velvet's shoulder, and the other he wrapped around her body, pressing his hand on the small of her back. Her flesh was warm to the touch.

The tent was almost complete in its stiff ascension.

She gently put a hand on his shoulder, wrapping the other around his waist. She pressed her head into his chest. Wrapped in each other's arms, they slowly rotated three hundred and sixty degrees to the Rolling Stones—*All the dreams we held so close seemed to all go up in smoke ... Let me whisper in your ear*—before Velvet whispered, "There's something wrong."

"I know," Nathan whispered. "I want to fuck your brains out." His cheeks flushed. He felt stupid after saying it. But he couldn't help himself. It had been over a month since he'd been laid and, being watched and listened to around the clock, even the palm sisters had tacitly indicated an unwillingness to come out and play. But now, this overpowering feeling of love—*no, lust*—superseded any apprehensions about what George Orwell in his novel *1984* had accurately called the Thought Police. He didn't care who was watching and what they were doing behind the scenes—even if they were having a double-fisted date with *their* palm sisters.

In this moment, Nathan's life had been reduced to one simple carnal objective—fuck.

"I feel it, too," Velvet whispered, pushing her crotch into his erection and rubbing softly. "That's what's wrong. I have no control over it."

Nathan moaned softly. "Velvet ... it's been a while since we—"

"Fucked?"

"Right."

"I remember ... I hope you don't think that meant anything?"

"No."

"Ahhh ... ahhhhhh ... ahhhhhhhhhh," she moaned, thrusting her crotch into his—harder, faster, harder, faster.

"What should we ... do?" Nathan asked. "Oooooooohhhhh ... that's good ... yeah."

The clothing-protected humping continued. "Ahhh ... ahhhh ... ahhhh ... ahhhhhh ... we're doing it," she said softly.

Then she started tearing his button-down shirt off—buttons popping and rolling on the floor—and Nathan pulled her blouse up over her head, pushed the black lace bra up and ravenously fondled the perky objects of his desire. He brought his tongue to an erect nipple, licked and sucked while Velvet moaned softly, moving a hand to his crotch and massaging his erection.

She stopped. "Wait."

Nathan's breath came in short gasps. "What?"

Velvet peeled her blouse all the way off, and tossed it at the monitor, where it snagged, blocking the lens. "No point in giving the voyeurs a free show."

There was another camera in another corner of the white room and Nathan took his cue, peeling off his shirt and slinging it up to the mechanical eye. The shirt dropped to the floor. He tried again. On the third shot it finally clung to the camera lens, offering them a modicum of privacy—at least visually. They knew they could still be heard, but didn't much care right now.

Velvet sat on the bed, rapidly undressing. As he approached, Nathan grinned and made a show of removing his pants, twirling them around like a male nude dancer for a few seconds before flinging them onto the table. The jeans struck the wine bottle and it rolled off the table, crashing onto the polished concrete floor, shattering, splattering red wine. Nathan ignored it, gyrating his hips like a male stripper and slowly removing his briefs.

Velvet, nude, watched and approved. "Get your ass over here already."

Grinning, Nathan twirled his black boxer briefs. He finished the show, tossing them into a corner. Then he dove on Velvet, the solid steel tent pole fully revealed, stiff and ready.

Chapter Six

Melvin was ready. Freshly shaved and showered, wearing new white coveralls, he wanted to find Larynda. He wanted to fuck Larynda. Where the hell was she and why wasn't Doctor Imes coming clean with him?

Sick? Don't think, do.

All Melvin could remember was Imes announcing the date, setting up the time and place, but no goddamned delivery. He knew his mind was flitting between rational and irrational thought—some psychosis stretching dark, mind-altering tendrils through his brain—but surely he would remember if he saw her.

Surely he would remember fucking her. That was something Melvin never forgot, even though he had added over a hundred notches to the babe belt since graduating high school in Prince Edward Island. And his job as a junk hauler had given him plenty of opportunity to do just that. It was easy. Pull in with the pick-up truck in the heat of summer, start loading in debris, get sweat-soaked, take off your shirt, revealing a lean, muscular body and then kindly knock on the door and ask for a glass of water. If the home was occupied by a divorced, widowed or infidelity-prone woman whose husband was at work (maybe out west, as they called it, working on the oil rigs) and wouldn't mind some carnal extracurricular activities, well then Melvin's smooth-talking charm would take care of the rest. It usually did.

But Melvin never told. Oh no. That's what kept him in business—the business of getting *his* junk off and getting *the*

39

junk loaded into the truck. He would often get a large tip and so would the pleasure-seeking women—all eight erect inches of it. He knew PEI was small—population 140,000-odd thousand—and word would spread like a wind-whipped bushfire if he ever opened his mouth. But he kept it shut.

And miraculously, the women had kept their mouths shut too, and Melvin's junk business had prospered. He suspected word got out at the odd hen party, but the gossiping gabbers seemed to keep it confined to hen parties—to horny, married, widowed, divorced, lonely women. Melvin imagined big-titted Bethel Dobson telling ornery but attractive Ellie Street that, "If you want to get fucked good, call Mel. He did me for over an hour. I had five orgasms—service with a smile. Call Mel. He delivers."

The wall intercom squawked, snapping Melvin from his reverie, forcing him to concentrate on the task at hand. It wasn't easy with the dark tendrils of psychosis growing, reaching, gradually enveloping his mind. *What the fuck is wrong with me?*

Steve Trimble's voice: "Melvin, I'm coming in with your dinner."

His muscles tensed. *Melting Pot! Why doesn't anyone call me fucking Melting Pot? That's a good one. Fucking Melting Pot. Get it? You're Melvin, idiot.*

"Okay."

The door opened and Steve wheeled a tray in, parking it beside a small desk where Melvin sat.

"You feeling better?" Steve asked, rubbing a hand through a mop of blonde hair.

Most of the crew sported crew cuts. Melvin didn't know how Steve got away with the hippie look. "I'm good, Steve. What's for dinner?"

Steve lifted a metal lid from the tray theatrically. "Spanish chicken, mashed potatoes and sautéed mush—"

Melvin lurched up from the chair, tackling him to the bed. The metal tray lid flew from his hand and clattered along the floor. Melvin quickly removed the cuffs dangling from Steve's belt, along with a large ring of keys. He twisted Steve's arm behind his back and forced him face-down into a pillow.

"What the fuck?" Steve said.

"Shut up. Which key is for the handcuffs?"

"You'll never get away with—"

Melvin twisted the arm at a painful angle. Steve let out a scream of pain.

"Which one?"

"The black one."

Dangling the keychain in front of a pained expression, he asked, "And the door?"

Silence—broken by a short, shrill scream after more arm wrenching.

"Which one opens the door?"

"Red ... the red one."

Melvin unlocked the handcuffs and then locked Steve's wrist to a steel bedpost. He then searched Steve's pockets, removing a cell phone and some odd black pager or tracking device. He put them in his coveralls pocket. "Don't worry. I'm not going to hurt you. I'm going to find Larynda. I'm as horny as a polecat. I need to get laid. Bad."

"You're not going to find Larynda," Steve said as Melvin opened the door.

"Why not?"

"She's dead. You killed her."

Chapter Seven

I hope he doesn't kill her, Doctor Imes thought, watching a live streaming video of *Nathan does Velvet Violently* from a small computer monitor in his office. The image on the screen showed Nathan pounding furiously into Velvet doggie-style while she moaned and screamed, at times as if in pain. Nathan had his head tilted at an odd angle and grinned maniacally. His face and body glistened with sweat.

Even the good doctor was getting aroused. Rather unsuccessful with women, he planned a rendezvous a little later with palm-sister-left, or Lisa as he preferred to call her, and palm-sister-right, or Reama as she was affectionately known. He grabbed his drink, a glass of Glenlivet single-malt scotch on the rocks, swallowed a mouthful, and set it down on the desk. He grinned, enjoying the on-screen action.

Although Imes wasn't a big drinker, tonight he had good reason to celebrate. The increased dosage of P-744 added to the wine had done the trick. The love part of the drug was working like a charm, even better than expected. Commander Stiessman was watching the same real-life porn show right now and, for all Imes knew, was on a date with his palm sisters or whatever he called them. Imes had called Stiessman when Nathan and Velvet had blocked the cameras and the wine bottle shattered, wanting the commander's permission to intervene. But Stiessman had switched on another secret camera hidden in the room's sprinkler system and warned Imes to "stay put and observe." A few minutes later, video restored,

Stiessman had called and offered a conditional congratulations "subject to how this session ends."

A built-in monitor beeped and Imes jumped, almost spilling the scotch on his keyboard. It was Commander Stiessman and the red light on the screen said urgent. He clicked a remote. "Yes sir," Imes stammered.

"We've got a problem," Stiessman said.

Nathan and Velvet grunted, moaned and groaned in the background.

"Oh ... you don't like the sex, sir?"

The commander narrowed his eyes. "I'm not talking about that. Zero-one was spotted wandering around Sector 17."

"Melvin escaped?"

"Yes. The test subject is loose on the ship. And it's your responsibility, Doctor Imes. I've dispatched three guards—including Corporal Rice Sterling—to retrieve him. They've been ordered to shoot to kill if he resists."

"You can't kill him."

"Like hell I can't. You assured me you were making progress, and now this. Zero-one is your responsibility, doctor. I suggest—no, I order you—to forget that celebratory drink and get your ass down to Sector 17 ASAP. Do I make myself clear?"

"Yes sir."

The screen faded to black.

Imes grabbed a Colt 45 handgun out of his desk drawer, stuffed it in his white lab-coat pocket, stood up, and glanced back at the porn show one last time before leaving. The image showed Velvet deep-throating Nathan while he sat on the bed and moaned. At least they had settled down.

Walking briskly through the corridors, Imes thought Stiessman had sent Sterling just to piss him off. Sterling had been undermining Imes's efforts ever since boarding the ship two months ago. The animosity went further back than that. Before the nuclear holocaust, Imes was a practicing physician in Charlottetown, PEI. Sterling's young wife, Milena, had come in one day complaining of a cough. It had been a busy day and Imes had been stressed over the recent separation from his wife, Elaine, who was threatening to take every penny of the doctor's hard-earned money: estate house, forty-six-foot yacht, even his Mercedes Benz. Imes had diagnosed Milena with the flu and sent her away with a cough-syrup prescription. Two weeks later, she had returned. Another cough-syrup prescription. Two months later, she had gotten a second opinion. A lung scan revealed a cancerous tumor. Four months later Milena, who did not respond favorably to chemotherapy or radiation treatment, died after the disease of death invaded her brain.

Sterling had never forgiven the doctor for his misdiagnosis. He had stormed into Imes's office one busy Friday afternoon, brandishing a pistol. "You killed my wife, now it's your turn."

But Sterling didn't kill him. He just pistol-whipped him in the head, leaving a three-inch gash on the doctor's forehead that required stitches. Imes bore the scar as a grim reminder of his incompetence and shame, like the scarlet A worn by convicted adulteress Hester Pryne in Nathaniel Hawthorne's novel *The Scarlet Letter.*

Imes never bothered pressing charges. He felt sympathy for Sterling, felt his pain, felt bad about the misdiagnosis, even though his medical mind reasoned it probably wouldn't have

mattered if he had ordered a lung scan during the initial
consultation with Milena. She had stage-four lung cancer.
There is no stage five. It was a death sentence he probably could
not have prevented.

But that hadn't stopped Sterling, a muscle-bound hulk of
a man, from badmouthing him in the community and causing
his business to drop by 60 per cent at a time when his ex was
taking aim at his fortune.

Imes frowned, rubbing the scar on his forehead as he
waited for an elevator that would take him to Sector 17.
Touching it always reminded him of the misdiagnosis, the
animosity—their mutual dislike for one another. The shame of
it all.

Stiessman knew of the acrimonious history and seemed to
pit the two against each other at every turn, putting more fuel
in an already blazing inferno of hate.

The elevator door opened and Imes put a hand to the cold
steel of the handgun. He hoped he wouldn't have to use it.
But with Sterling, you could never be sure. Imes had witnessed
Sterling—loose cannon with a loose trigger finger—put a
bullet in the head of one innocent test subject already.

The door closed. The elevator whirred mechanically and
rapidly descended three floors. It stopped at Sector 17, a
myriad of offices, dormitories and hallways. Test subjects and
staff were housed here.

Nathan and Velvet were here, fucking like rabbits.

As soon as he stepped out, Imes heard the commotion at
the far end of a whitewashed, well-lit hallway. He moved down
the hall and stopped when he reached the altercation.

Two soldiers—Imes recognized them as Tig Landry and Marcus Sling—stood behind Sterling, training modified AK-47s at Melvin's head while Sterling stood over him with a gun, pistol-whipping his Melvin Melon repeatedly. The weapon dripped blood. Sterling's hands were painted dark red and Melvin's face was cut and bleeding, a bloody smear around his lips creating the image of a freakish, eerily grinning clown.

Melvin groaned as he was beaten, the sounds growing fainter. He was very near unconsciousness or death.

Imes stood twenty feet away from the macabre spectacle. He hated the sight of blood. He felt an acidic liquid push its way up his esophagus. He swallowed hard and put a hand in a pocket, touching the reassuring steel of the handgun. "That's enough, Sterling."

Landry lowered his weapon and turned around, facing Imes, while Sling kept his gun trained on Melvin, who continued receiving blows from the handgun. His groans had become a soft, nasally wheezing sound.

Faint, pleasurable moaning sounds could be heard a few doors down—two bodies in the throes of passion and lust.

Louder: "I said that's enough!"

Sterling stopped, whirling around to face Imes. A small cut on the bridge of his nose snaked rivulets of blood down his face, onto and into his mouth. He, too, was starting to resemble a demonic clown. Sterling wiped a fresh drop of dark red blood off his lips. "Hell if it is. Your lunatic here punched me in the nose."

"Release him into my custody," Imes ordered. He massaged his weapon.

"Are you trying to pull rank on me?"

"As senior doctor on this ship, I am pulling rank on you."

"You think you outrank me?"

"The test subjects are my responsibility."

Sterling stepped back from his victim, whose breathing had become more labored. "If they behave themselves, they're your responsibility, Imes. This one's not behaving himself. I've been ordered to shoot to kill if he displayed any resistance." He brought a hand to his nose, a little crooked as the result of Melvin's blow. "I think this qualifies as resistance. That little fuck broke my nose."

Imes looked at Landry and Sling for support. Sling had lowered his weapon. Both men watched Imes wearily. "You two, help me get him to the infirmary. Sterling, go take care of your nose, please."

"I'll take care of *your* nose, you self-righteous fuck." Sterling raised the pistol high in the air and charged at Imes. It happened so fast that instead of reaching for his gun, Imes brought both hands up to his face in defense.

The weapon connected with his forearm but the momentum of Sterling's charge bowled Imes over. Sterling landed on top of Imes. Wearing a maniacal grin, Sterling raised the pistol for another strike.

Imes, a much smaller man, wasn't much of a fighter. He closed his eyes tightly and covered them with his forearms. "Nooooo ... noooooo ... nooooooo!"

He felt the sting of the pistol grip as it repeatedly struck his forearm.

"I gave you a little scar last time, you shit ... now you're going to get much more than that. I'm going to split your stupid little head wide o—"

A built-in speaker on the corridor wall squawked: "That's enough, Corporal Sterling." It was Commander Stiessman.

******

Sterling's handgun-wielding hand froze and he looked up at the speaker. The promotion. He wanted that promotion almost as much as he wanted to end Imes's life. And, now, in an uncontrollable fit of rage, he might have ruined it all. He holstered the weapon, stood up and stepped away from Imes. He knew the commander could see everything on the monitors. "I'm sorry, sir."

The commander did not acknowledge the apology. "Landry and Sling—help Doctor Imes and zero-one to the infirmary. Sterling, I want to see you in my office. ASAP!"

Chapter Eight

ASAP, Nathan thought, overhearing Stiessman's words. *As soon as possible. What a stupid acronym. Like someone else's time is more valuable than yours ... that they have no respect for your time. And doesn't it also suggest an emergency? As soon as possible doesn't mean an emergency necessarily, but hasn't it evolved to mean just that? It's never good, that's for sure. If someone asked me to do something ASAP I'd stall as long as possible before dealing with them. Fuck them, and fuck their ASAP.*

Velvet had made an improvised dustpan and broom from a dinner plate and toilet paper. She cleaned up the spilled and shattered remains of the wine and bottle. "Did you hear that?"

Nathan lay in bed.

Over the music and their pleasurable moaning, Nathan had thought he heard muted thumping, conversation, and even cries of pain just down the hall. But the sex had taken precedence and he had put it out of his mind as nothing. In the end, he couldn't be sure. But the ASAP? Where had it come from? Had he heard it? Yes. It came from a loudspeaker?

"Do you mean ASAP?" he asked.

"Yeah."

"I hate that acronym."

"Did you hear it?"

"I think I did."

Velvet cleaned up the last of the broken mess, dumped it into a garbage can and returned. "Get dressed. We need to talk."

Nathan got out of bed, retrieved his clothing, including the articles that had concealed the cameras, put on his underwear and went into the bathroom. He closed the door, dressed, and ran some water in the vanity sink. He heard a knock on the bathroom door.

"Let me in," Velvet said.

He opened the door. She stepped inside, turning the vanity taps on high. She also turned the shower taps on full, hoping the sound of water splashing would drown out the conversation. She closed the door and faced Nathan as the small bathroom began clouding with steam.

Her face glistened with sweat and condensation. Strands of her black hair clung to her forehead. "Listen," she whispered, moving closer to Nathan. "Let's get a few things straight. First, keep your voice down. I'm sure this bathroom is wired. Second, that sex was good. I'm not going to lie. But it was only that—sex. It means nothing to me. It doesn't mean we're going to become an item and live happily ever after."

"Okay." Nathan was a little dumbfounded by her aggressive tone.

She continued. "The other thing: it wasn't real."

"It sure felt real."

"I'm not talking about that. It was drug-induced. They're brainwashing us. Can't you tell?"

Nathan scratched his head-stubble. "I suppose you're right."

"I know I'm right. I know how my head operates and this isn't me. It's the fucking drug, whatever it is. One minute I'm horny, the next pissed off—alternating between a love-hate relationship with myself and society, or what's left of it. You said it yourself earlier. You're up and down, all over the map. Horny, aggressive, happy, sad, all that."

"But I have other issues. Memory issues."

"But you heard the commotion outside? What the fuck are they doing to the other survivors? There are too many unanswered questions. Who dropped the bomb, who is responsible for the follow-up biological weapon? If we're supposed to be infected, how come no one's wearing fucking hazmat suits? This isn't quarantine we're in. We're caged rats and they're playing with our minds."

"What do you propose we do about it? We're supposed to hear all about it tomorrow. Imes said Stiessman will tell us about District 101, tell us what happened. Make things transparent."

"Transparent? There's no such thing as transparency with the government. What planet were you born on? There's always an agenda. Don't you know that by now?"

Nathan thought at one time he did know it. It was either the amnesia or the drug affecting his mind, dulling his reasoning powers, making him want to conform and tow the party line. "You have a plan?"

She pointed to her waist, where the black handle of a military combat knife protruded. "When Imes arrives, I'm going to lock him in the room and we'll get the hell out of here."

"And do what? The ship's crawling with cameras and soldiers. Do you really think they'll let us escape?"

"I have to try. You heard that commotion?"

Nathan wasn't sure anymore, so he just shook his head.

"I didn't think so," Velvet said. "While you were napping, I had my ear pinned to the door. They were beating someone. I think Sterling was beating someone. They brainwash you, maybe it doesn't work, than they kill you. I'm not letting that happen. I'd rather die fighting than bend to some government plan for a controlled, docile and patriotic population. I'm getting out of here."

"I don't know, Velvet. You're not thinking rationally. You'll never make it."

She touched the handle of the knife. "Either you're with me or against me. And make up your mind quick. This isn't some government committee meeting, where I'll wait two weeks for a report on your findings."

A buzzer sounded. Someone was at the door. Buzzing out of courtesy. They could enter at will. The captives had no real privacy and hardly even an illusion of it. Imes's voice: "You decent? Can I come in?"

"What's it going to be?" Velvet asked.

Nathan stared at her blankly. He didn't want to commit to something he thought was ludicrous. If there was a drug, it was skewing the way Velvet processed information. He was sure she never would have made such a harebrained plan in the past. Her performance on PEI, although brave, wasn't stupid. *Except when she decided to go for that stupid picture ... that's why you no longer have a soulmate. Velvet's responsible for her murder.* Maybe her plans were stupid? "Sorry. You're on your own on this one."

"You won't interfere?"

"No ... but I'm not helping."

The door whirred metallically and opened. The time for talk was over. Nathan hoped against all hope that Velvet wasn't about to do something stupid.

Velvet left the bathroom. He turned off the taps and followed.

Imes stood inside, looking fatigued. He fidgeted with something in his pocket. His brow was creased with worry lines and red welts covered his forearm.

He was alone. *Where are the guards?* Nathan thought. Imes didn't generally enter without armed protection. A breach of protocol. What was wrong?

Velvet moved in close, a hand wandering down to her waistline.

"I hope you enjoyed your ... little meeting," Imes said, a faint pink blush crawling up his cheeks. "I see you covered the video cameras. But ... everyone's entitled to privacy."

"Privacy ... what privacy?" Nathan asked, while Velvet inched closer.

Imes sensed the intrusion to his personal circle of deference and stepped back, a hand slipping into a lab-coat pocket.

Nathan noticed the hand, thought he saw the outline of a gun behind the fabric, and continued: "We've been held like laboratory animals for what ... a month now, and we're not getting any answers, doc. What the fuck gives?"

"I have answers," Imes said, taking another step back. "District 101 is ready. We're taking you there tomorrow. You'll be free."

Velvet stopped.

Imes continued: "You have to understand. We have your best interests at heart. Always have. We just had to be sure you weren't infected." There was a pleading look in his eyes, a you-have-to-believe-me tone to the words.

"When is Stiessman going to fill us in?" Nathan asked.

"That was set for tonight, but the commander had some important business that came up. You'll both be meeting with him tomorrow afternoon at one."

"Is that a gun in your pocket or are you just happy to see us?" Velvet asked with a mocking smirk.

Imes looked frazzled. "This isn't the love boat, you know."

"Could have fooled me," Velvet said, wiping a sweaty brow. "Our session would rival the best porn on the internet. What's with the gun? Don't trust us anymore?"

"A virus-infected civilian is losing his faculties. There was an incident." Imes withdrew the handgun, holding it barrel-up like a lawyer might present Exhibit A. "It was just for my protection. I didn't have to use it and everything's fine now. The man's going to be okay."

"Going to be okay?" Velvet asked. "Is that the beating we heard in the hall? What did you do to him?"

"I didn't do anything. I'm just trying to help. I'm a doctor. I heal people, not hurt them."

A pause.

Nathan saw Velvet's hand move closer to the knife. She took a small step toward Imes, who this time stood his ground.

We behave ourselves and we get out of here, Nathan thought. *We don't and we get killed.* Nathan slid an arm around Velvet, kissing her on the cheek and whispering in her ear: "No ... please." Louder: "Honey, do you want to sleep in my room tonight?"

******

Velvet felt an urge to recoil but a wave of rational thought invaded her drug-induced mind. She casually released the knife and wrapped an arm around Nathan's waist. "Thanks for the invite, baby, but not tonight. I don't know if they'd allow it anyway, and I want a good night's sleep for our release tomorrow." Pecking Nathan on the cheek, "I'm so looking forward to getting off this ship and getting back on land ... a free woman." She was beaming and didn't know if Imes could tell just how plastic the whole charade actually was.

Imes looked at the happy couple. His eyes said it all: *That's it. Play along, even if you don't believe it. Behave yourself if you want off this ship. Think about it.*

Chapter Nine

Nathan didn't know why he had started thinking about Edward Sole. Ed was dead, had sacrificed his life courageously battling the murderous Neanderthals so Nathan could escape on a fishing boat, only to find himself on another floating vessel nervously awaiting an unknown fate. But maybe it was because in death, Ed had given Nathan a new life. Maybe that was why the maniacally grinning, insane face of Ed had popped into Nathan's mind. Maybe it was also because Commander Stiessman sat at the head of a boardroom table, a half-dozen armed guards at his side, extolling the virtues of this new life.

While Stiessman talked, Imes and Velvet listened intently. Nathan only half-listened, even though his future or lack thereof was on the line, he struggled to piece together the Ed image. Was it an Ed epiphany?

Stiessman continued: "Think of District 101, or 101 as we call it, as your little utopia. A new beginning. A place to heal, to rebuild, to find some happiness while we work with the US government and the US military, to restore order to the rest of the world. We have issues to deal with before you can be released back into civilization. It'll be at least another six months—maybe a year—before radiation levels will be safe for human habitation. Not to mention there are some savage groups we're still exterminating."

"What about the zombies?" Velvet asked.

"We're still working on that. You see, after North Korea dropped the nuke, they followed it up with a biological weapon. This man-made virus was meant to mutate and kill, but somehow it mixed with the radiation and created some sort of walking-dead phenomena that Doctor Imes is still studying."

The image of Ed flashed in Nathan's mind again and he realized its context. He had dreamed of Ed last night. Again. In the dream, Nathan was watching a kids' soccer game on a summer day in PEI. The sidelines were crowded. Ed was beside him and they cheered along a little boy as he made a breakaway with the ball, kicked it high and left, out of reach of the goalie, and into the net. A goal. The sidelines erupted with cheers and Nathan felt warm hands on his back, caressing and hugging. The hands stopped and a small, short-haired woman pressed tightly against him, her hands wrapped around his waist.

Nathan glanced back. She was attractive enough: small features, a cheerful smile. He turned back to the soccer game. Then the dread, dull at first, then coursing through his body like freezing rain. He knew why. The unknown woman caressing him from behind was poisoning him. Her hands—her entire body—were laced with poison and it was now on his clothing and would surely seep into his bloodstream and that would be that. The end. Do not pass go, do not collect two hundred dollars.

He turned to the woman. "Please take your hands off me."

She looked at him curiously. "What for? I like you."

Then Ed grabbed him by the arm. "We have to go. She's trying to kill you. We have to go. Now!"

As they ran through the open fields in fear, the blue sky turned dark red, gray, and finally black. "Do you know where we're going?" Nathan asked as they ran. Then he noticed Ed didn't look the same; not anything like how Nathan had remembered him, defending the cave against The Neanderthals a month or so ago. Then, his face had been streaked with dark red blood, lines extending from his nose and spreading out across his cheeks. They had been attacked by the mutant seagulls, and Ed had been left with a half-dozen V-shaped cuts on his face from the fiercely pecking birds. Instead of cleaning the wounds, Ed had smeared the blood, mixed with dirt, across his face in odd-shaped lines—a warrior painting his face, a pre-battle ritual. He had looked insane the last time Nathan saw him. But in the dream, he looked like the Ed of old, normal as normal could be.

"I thought you knew," Ed said.

They both stopped, caught their breaths, evidently free of the poison woman.

"Are you okay?" Ed asked.

Nathan didn't feel any poison coursing through his body. Not yet, anyway. "I feel fine."

"And you know where to go?"

"I do know." Nathan withdrew some business cards from a pocket. He produced a business card and showed it to Ed.

Ed nodded. "The Olde Dublin Pub in Charlottetown. That's it. Let's go for a beer."

"Sounds good." Somehow, at that moment, it seemed the most perfectly natural thing in the world to do. More than that, it seemed like the only thing to do at the time.

But then the intermittent melodious chirps of swallows turned to the cawing of crows, then loud screeching seagulls—mutant killer seagulls—coming like a wave, a thick white mass descending down from the black curtain of night. Nathan covered his face with his arms, legs firmly planted in the grass, immobilized, as the angry birds found their prey and poked, pecked and sliced his flesh from his face, tearing it off in large ribbon-like pieces ... *no, no, no.*

Nathan shuddered as the nightmare's images evaporated. "What about the birds?" he said, hands trembling, staring at Stiessman, wide-eyed.

Imes looked at him concernedly. "Are you okay? Your face is as white as a ghost."

"Just a bad nightmare. What about the birds?"

"We do have concerns about mutated and infected animal species," Stiessman said. "But 101 is sealed off from the outside world. It's protected by a high-tech glass dome. You'll be safe until we can get exterior dangers neutralized and start to rebuild infrastructure outside. Maybe one day you'll even be able to return home."

"Why didn't we get infected?" Velvet asked. "Nathan and I got bitten by seagulls. We're not zombies."

Imes said, "There are a number of people who didn't—in layman's terms—turn. They're immune. Nathan and you are immune to the virus. I don't know why yet, but I'm working on it. But you're not immune to radiation, and that's why we had to administer P-744, the anti-radiation drug. And we had to keep you quarantined to be absolutely sure you didn't get infected with the virus and start a little rumble of your own on the ship. In some cases we've seen, the virus can incubate for as long as a month."

Velvet didn't look entirely satisfied with the answer. "What about you guys?" She waved a hand at the others and pointed to Stiessman. "All of you? You're all immune?"

"Our intelligence sources learned of North Korea's development of EZ-6 some time ago," Stiessman said. "We managed to get a sample of it, develop a vaccine and vaccinate all important medical personnel, soldiers, government officials, etcetera."

Velvet's eyes narrowed. "So you get to play God?"

"Someone's got to," Stiessman said. "It was in the interest of national security that we inoculate people who could supervise the rebuilding of our country, should it come to that. We never saw the need to inoculate the general populous ... never in a million years did we think the North Koreans would deploy EZ-6, never mind the nuclear bomb."

Velvet's face flushed, eyes narrowing. She opened her mouth to speak. Nathan flashed a look—shut up—and she closed her mouth without saying a word.

"What's the state of the world now?" Nathan asked. "How many people left, how many countries haven't been blown to shit or attacked with bio-weapons?"

Stiessman said, "From what we can gather, there are pockets of Asia, including North Korea, still intact—pockets of Russia, a few Caribbean islands. Small parts of Canada and the United States have also been preserved due to our high level of preparedness. Initial estimates put the death toll at close to 7 billion, a few hundred million shy of the entire world population. But these estimates are preliminary. With infrastructures and much of modern technology destroyed, it's hard to be sure. We do know, with the infection rate of EZ-6, radiation poisoning, and the formation of savage tribes, that the number of dead increases substantially every day. To put it another way, we're in a pile of shit. But we're working around the clock to fix it. I'm not at liberty to say much more right now." The last sentence was delivered with a tone of finality.

Imes stood, gesturing with a wave to Velvet and Nathan. "Let's go. We have a chopper ready. We're taking you to 101."

Chapter Ten

Four days later, Nathan realized 101 wasn't anything like he imagined. He had thought his movements would be tightly controlled, with closed circuit TVs positioned everywhere, armed soldiers closely watching them, and Doctor Imes delivering daily injections of what he now knew as P-744, the so-called anti-radiation drug. He had imagined a sterile, hospital-like environment. But as he sat at the kitchen table of a comfortable steel home, eating a green sludge—*Soylent Green is people*—which Imes had assured him would restore his fitness level, looking out the small window at the infinite although glass-encased sea view, 101 almost seemed like a paradise: lush vegetation, trees, and a row of greenhouses sprouting a variety of vegetables. Even his one-bedroom corrugated metal home was painted in contemporary dark green tones.

Sure, Imes had visited—what, twice in four days?—but only to ask questions about how Nathan was adjusting to the new world order, and more importantly how he was feeling. Nathan had told the doctor fine, but on the last visit had finally admitted to the troubling nightmares. Nightmares that had intensified in ferocity and frequency. And recently they seemed to involve women, women who wanted to harm or kill him. And Ed, always Ed, trying to save him from the clutches of the evil women.

"I think I have the answer," Imes had said on his last visit, producing the photo of Nathan's parents he had promised. Examining the photo, Nathan saw his father Thomas, a sixtyish man with a thick head of shortly-cropped gray hair standing in a backyard, a two-story wooden house in the background. Thomas had his arm around his wife Anna's shoulder. She held a rake in one hand. She was smiling for the camera. They were average-looking parents with worn-out clothes. They could have been anyone's lower middle class parents. Some memories had materialized in Nathan's mind. *They're my parents, but what of it? Were they good or bad? I have no idea.*

Imes seemed to read Nathan's mind. "I can see you recognize them." He set a newspaper clipping on the table. Nathan read the headline, *Woman Convicted in Stabbing Death of Husband.* There was a picture of Anna, dressed in orange prison overalls, arms and legs shackled in chains, her face downcast, being led out of the courtroom by two sheriffs. Another picture showed Thomas grinning ear to ear, as if welcoming death. The end of his life had come as the result of 44 stab wounds at Anna's hands.

Nathan cringed as a tidal wave of terrible memories washed over him. A collage of images: Thomas yelling at Anna, striking Anna, violent arguing. In one surreal image, Nathan remembered talking back to his father, telling him in no uncertain terms he didn't want a crew cut. He liked his long hair just the way it was. His father had exploded in anger. Nathan sprinted down the street, Thomas in hot pursuit, brandishing a leather belt—The Strap—and yelling, "Come back here, you little shit, and face the music. Only cowards run from punishment. Come back, come—"

The twisted collage evaporated slowly as Imes put a reassuring hand on Nathan's shoulder. "It's okay. You blocked those memories after the amnesia-producing fall. But your nightmares are related to your parents. You're afraid you'll become like your father—abusive and disrespectful to women—maybe you think you're already like him. I hate to be so blunt, but your mother killed him. If you see yourself as following in his footsteps, wouldn't women want to kill you? Why do you think all the women in your dreams want to kill you? Why do you think those dreams are so frightening? You're afraid to die, and maybe you think you deserve to die, if you're like Thomas."

"I'm not like Thomas," Nathan blurted out, covering his hands with his face.

"Well then, carry on. Now you know more than ever what not to do. And I encourage you to see Velvet. Why do you refuse to see her?"

Nathan wondered if Velvet's decision to return to her house prior to escaping PEI—a decision that had cost Cadence her life—had anything to do with his avoidance of Velvet of late. He didn't know. He was confused. "I had coffee with her when we first got here."

"Nathan, that was a five-minute visit. I thought you were establishing a close bond with Velvet."

Contemplating his behavior, Nathan shoveled the last tablespoonful of green sludge into his mouth. He fought an urge to pick up the newspaper article and the photo on the table where he had tossed it an hour ago after Imes's visit. Why had he been avoiding Velvet? She lived nearby in an identical steel bungalow-style home. He had watched her leave every morning at seven, climb on her government-issued mountain bike, and cycle around 101 for an hour before returning home. She had on three occasions buzzed his doorbell, but he had ignored it.

And it hadn't been easy. Powerful and mysterious forces were at work—forces Nathan had little control over. There was a feeling of love or something approximating it, accompanied by the tingly sensation of arousal in his loins. These feelings may have been there before, but Nathan didn't remember them being as powerful as they were now.

It was like the government was trying to pair Nathan and Velvet, an arranged union after discovering they were friends with benefits and had watched each other's backs in life-and-death situations. Hell, they had been through more trauma and drama in a month than many people experienced in a thirty-year marriage. Was he afraid he was going to do something bad to her? Afraid he was becoming like Thomas? Maybe she would kill him for it?

The color drained from Nathan's face as he remembered his nightmare last night. He didn't realize he was gripping the edge of the table, white-knuckled, grinding his teeth. *What the fuck? That was Velvet's face, attacking me with ... no, oh no, oh baby no ... a knife!*

The sound interrupted the fury of his thoughts—the chirping that would soon be followed by the high-pitched screeching of the descending seagulls. The mutant bloodsuckers had continued to haunt his nightmares. He got up and rushed to the window. He was about to press the button that would close the mechanical blinds and muffle the noise when he recognized Velvet's mountain bike pass by, returning from her morning cycle. Nathan, unlike her, hadn't been able to lift a finger, never mind a body, to pick up the bike that stood on the front lawn leaning against the white picket fence.

Irrational, disconnected thoughts tumbled in a troubled mind: *Hell. Hell on Earth. Poison women, poison women. Poison me, poison me.*

He felt like Edward Sole must have when he finally lost complete control of his senses; insanity inserting a prominent and permanent foothold—or in this case, mindhold.

Get a grip, you fucking loser. Talk to her. He quickly went to the door and swung it open. The screeching was getting louder. Velvet had dismounted the bike and was propping it up against the fence. "Velvet?"

She looked at him. "Hey, stranger. Did I shit in your cornflakes? Or shit in your Soylent Green?"

"Sorry," Nathan said, stepping off the porch and approaching. "I was just sorting out some shit. Can we talk?"

"Maybe Soylent Green gave you diarrhea. Remember what Charlton Heston said: 'Soylent Green is people.' And people don't agree with you."

Nathan stood on the sidewalk about twenty feet from Velvet when the bird bloodbath commenced.

They looked up at the white mass descending on the glass dome. Hazy gray-orange clouds covered the sky. Crimson-colored spears of light poked through. It was like the sky was on fire and the sun was some demented pyromaniac supervising the blaze. En masse, the birds smashed into the glass dome, multiple clunking and clucking sounds and splashes of dark red as they tie-dyed the ceiling. Dead birds slid down the glass sides, snaked by slithery trails of blood.

"Painting the town red," Velvet said with a cynical smile.

Nathan grimaced, slowly removing his hands from his ears as the last squawk and splat echoed off the dome, a few remaining birds evidently heeding the grim reaper's warning and flying off into the eerie orange post-apocalyptic sunrise. He knew a military chopper would arrive soon to pressure-wash the mess of blood and entrails. He had seen it, heard it, been haunted by the ritual before.

Now they stood face-to-face, Velvet on the resident's side of the white picket fence, Nathan on the neighbor's side. "What's on your mind, cowboy?" she asked.

"I want to apologize for being so distant lately."

"You did that already."

"I mean it. I'm sorry. I don't know what got into me." Actually, Nathan had a pretty good idea now; he just didn't know if he wanted to talk about it here and now.

"Don't sweat it. Everyone's entitled to their own privacy. How's Imes been treating you?"

"Actually, I find him quite helpful."

"Do you?" Velvet's eyes narrowed. She moved closer and whispered: "I wouldn't take that to the bank."

"He's helping. Some of my memory is coming back—my parents." Maybe he did want to talk about it here and now. "I know what you're thinking ... that they're trying to con—"

Velvet pointed to her front door. "Hey, wanna join me for a coffee?"

"Sure."

******

A few minutes later, sipping hot coffee in white mugs, Nathan heard the familiar sound—wop-wop-wop-wop—of chopper rotors above, realizing with a heavy sigh it meant seagull blood and guts were being power-washed off glass. Until the rotors started, Velvet had kept the conversation about day-to-day observations, telling Nathan she had overheard two soldiers discussing the arrival of a new resident, one Melvin Tierney, who would apparently be located next door to Nathan, residence PB-3 in Sector B.

She told him about other things she had noticed: an educational wing, hospital complex, a sophisticated power generation system, air purification and temperature-control machinery, command post, military compound, weapon and vehicle arsenal, a structure of water wells and a livestock farming wing where she had noticed multiple animal species—absent in the dome were the birds, who weren't behaving themselves lately.

But once the chopper rotors sounded, her tone turned serious. She slid her chair close to Nathan, put an arm around his shoulder and spoke in a hushed tone, her lips two inches from his ear.

"You don't think they're trying to control us? Give your clouded head a shake. Do you think they would have all this organized—thought through in advance—if they weren't planning something like this?"

Velvet smelled of roses and honey, a fragrant aroma that caused a faint stirring in Nathan's loins. *Not again!* "That doesn't mean anything," he said. "All it means is our military, our government, was ready for such an attack. Think about it. In our current state of chaos, don't you think it would behoove our government—in the interest of national security—to prepare for the worst in the advent of a nuclear bomb, chemical attack, bio-weapon, whatever?"

"Are you telling me you believe the North Koreans did all this?"

"Who else? Why would they lie to us?"

"I can think of a hundred reasons, not least of all because they want a population they can control. Have you thought about P-744 lately? How it makes you love, but at the same time makes you hate? Notice any side effects?" She touched his leg, and he felt his member rise and throb-throb-throb. "Are you horny again? Haven't you been a little too horny for a little too long? Or don't you realize it? Have you fully succumbed to P-744?"

Nathan tried to will the flagpole to half-mast. But it defied his orders and stood at full-mast, defiantly proclaiming its innocence. The thumping rotors—there must have been two choppers this time, Nathan thought grimly—grew fainter as the soldiers finished hosing off dead seagulls and headed for base.

Velvet removed her arm from Nathan's shoulder, extracted the walking finger from his pant leg, and pushed her chair back. She winked and took a sip of coffee. "So, tell me about your parents."

Ahh ... what the hell. Maybe I need to get this off my chest. Maybe it'll help me. If I give a little, maybe she'll give a little and I'll learn something about what makes her so confidently tough, so enigmatic, so goddamned sexy.

Nathan began apprehensively: "I hope you don't hold this against me ... but part of the reason I've been ... ahh ... non-communicative lately is I've been feeling this rage—rage that's directed at women. Sometimes it feels like it's boiling over. When I feel like that I need to be alone, you know, try and contain it."

Nathan told her what he had found out about his parents. According to Doctor Imes's diagnosis, Nathan was afraid he was becoming a woman-hater like his father. And since he was starting to hate himself for hating women, he was being haunted by nightmares of women wanting to kill him. He finished the story, saying Imes had traced the personality disorder back to Nathan's childhood, a disorder that could be cured if he could realize that, although he was a product of his upbringing, he was also his own person in many ways and he could make a conscious choice to love women and understand that he was not his father and never would be.

"Quite the epiphany," Velvet said. "I'm not in any danger, am I?"

Although she had tried to deliver the comment flippantly, Nathan could see doubt in her eyes, perhaps mixed with a bit of sadness. Even if he chose to answer the question, he knew it would be a moot point. He knew Velvet well enough to realize fear was not a part of her DNA code. At least if it was, she hid it expertly. If she felt any threat at all from Nathan, she would mitigate the threat before it crystalized into action. And, depending on her mood, she would mitigate it with threats or physical violence.

That much he did understand.

He also realized in that moment that Velvet could probably wipe the floor with his ass if they ever squared off in hand-to-hand combat. She took pains to keep herself alert and in excellent physical health. Meanwhile, Nathan hadn't exercised in a week, wasn't sleeping well, and was dying for a shot of scotch that Imes had promised but had yet to deliver. Maybe even a smoke. Nathan wanted to wash his nightmares away in a trickling creek—no, a rushing river—of alcohol. *One drink ... surely one bottle couldn't hurt.*

Nathan shook his head. "No, Velvet, I could never hurt you." *Your nightmare ... it was her. She tried to kill you. Maybe she wants to kill you. If she wants to kill me what should I do? Kill her first. Banish the thought, you fucking nutcase ... banish the thought.*

"What I meant was, do you want to hurt me?" Velvet asked.

"No," Nathan said, unconvinced. "Tell me about your parents, then."

Velvet's face clouded. After a short pause, she began.

******

As she talked, she recalled the image of her drunken father, Jeritt Jones, bobbing his head, helplessly flailing arms, drowning, crying for help, while she repeatedly pushed him back down with an oar, drowning the pedophile, ending his miserable existence forever. Jeritt had sexually abused Velvet one too many times. And Velvet had decided to take the law into her own hands. That, after Velvet had complained to Margaret, her meek, subservient and yes, abused mother, and those same complaints had been answered with a reprimand ... "You're a bad girl for making up nasty stories about a decent man."

Jeritt's last words still echoed in Velvet's mind: "You'll never amount to shit ... you useless bitch." And perhaps those words would have haunted her had she not gotten the last word in just before Jerrit's head sunk underneath the ocean water off the coast of PEI for the very last time. "You *are* a piece of shit ... but your perverted shit-disturbing days are over." It was that comment that brought a smile to her face when she recalled the incident that had resulted in her father's death, estranged her mother, but had left her with a survivalist mentality and an inherent distrust of people, particularly men.

Her smile fading, she told Nathan that the police had chalked it up as a mere boating accident. And soon after, her mother had abandoned her, fled PEI to the province of Ontario, and Velvet was put into the care of her well-meaning but strict grandmother Emma, who had raised her from the tender but no longer innocent age of thirteen.

Velvet had learned how it felt to kill righteously.

And it felt good.

Completing the story, two things occurred to her: one, she *had* been thinking more often lately of the head-for-an-eye justice she had served to pedophile Jeritt. Two, where that memory had only brought her satisfaction in the past, it was now starting to haunt her and play with a psyche she had thought had come to grips with and adjusted to the trauma. *Why? Why am I thinking about it all now, reliving it? Why, no more satisfaction? How does it make me feel? I could kill someone ... no, no, no ...*

******

It was Nathan's hand reaching out and gently touching her arm that stopped her words, which had been bursting forth like popping kernels in a popcorn maker.

"Wow ... you've battled a lot. You're incredibly resilient," he said, searching her eyes, understanding why she was the way she was. But as Nathan said it, a terrible realization struck him. *My mother killed my father and Velvet killed her father. What a horrible irony—both of our fathers murdered. By macabre design.*

Velvet's expression changed. She was determined and confident once again, ready to take on the world. She touched Nathan's hand and raised her eyebrow. "Do you want to see my rose garden?"

The roses ... the honey ... the garden. "Okay."

She led him outside to the small garden. The grass was well-manicured. Velvet turned on a nearby hose and dragged it along as they walked across the lawn to a small cultivated circle at the left corner. There stood three healthy rose bushes with pink, yellow and red flowers. Beside them, a purple lilac bush bloomed. Next to that, some patches of bright, multi-colored chrysanthemums.

Funny, Nathan thought. *I never pictured Velvet as a gardener.*

As she watered the flowers with a fine mist, she began whispering: "I didn't want to say too much inside. I've tipped that place over looking for bugs and couldn't find a damn thing. But that doesn't mean we're not being watched and listened to. They're not to be trusted. Look what they did to us on the ship."

Nathan moved closer, tried a smile that didn't seem to work, and nodded.

Velvet continued: "Make it look good ... think of a romantic gesture. I know you're just dying to fuck me."

Nathan felt his face flush. He put an arm around her shoulder clumsily and kissed her on the cheek. He held her like that for a moment, feeling as awkward as a duck trying to walk a tightrope.

After an awkward silence, she said: "Haven't you figured it out yet? It's the P-744. I have to admit, I've been thinking the same things you have. For you, it's violence against women. For me, it's violence against men. The childhood stuff, the shit we thought we'd dealt with, is coming back to haunt us, causing us to behave in irrational ways. Who knows where it'll lead, but we've got to stop it."

As he listened and tried to make sense of Velvet's words, one part of Nathan's mind was thinking of how much he'd like to fuck this useless bitch to death. Accomplish the love and hate thing in one fell swoop.

Then, as the rational part of his mind slowly prevailed and he realized the insanity of his last thought, something else occurred to him. If P-744 was designed as a population-controlling drug, there was something its designers had evidently overlooked—something that could maybe be turned against them.

He said it out loud before realizing it: "Side effects. Nasty side effects."

Chapter Eleven

When he was designing trial batches of P-744, Doctor Imes thought he had witnessed all the nasty side effects. He had seen rhesus monkeys fucking like rabbits non-stop for four or more hours in a day, before collapsing from fatigue and sleeping another four hours. He had watched the rhesus monkeys direct violence against the handlers, spitting, throwing feces (Doctor Imes had twice been plastered with a chocolate mustache), scratching, biting and urinating everywhere. One monkey had even escaped from its cage, attacking and raking claws down Jeffrey Laines's face and damn near clawing his eyes clean out of their sockets.

And the painful cries echoing from monkey mouths as they received P-744 injections.

But nothing had prepared him for the sight that beheld his eyes now. George, his star pupil, was humping doggie-style a female monkey called Gina. George had a wild look in his eyes as he hammered away, completely oblivious to Imes's intrusion. Each thrust brought fresh squirts of blood from Gina's ravaged vagina. She lay on the metal cage floor limp, eyes wide open but lifeless, her left arm twisted at an odd angle. Evidently, George had broken the arm before or during intercourse. It wasn't clear. But one thing was clear.

George had fucked Gina to death.

Imes brought a hand to his mouth, fighting an urge to vomit. Although a chemical biologist and a general physician, Imes never did have a strong stomach when it came to violence and bloodshed; a bitter irony, considering his work of late.

Imes moved closer to the cage.

George hissed, continuing to hump the corpse.

"George ... stop that," Imes said.

George continued his monkey business without so much as a glance at Imes. He looked intent on fucking himself to death.

Then Imes remembered. There was code for this eventuality. There was a letter-number combination that in trials had stilled out-of-control violent impulses. Failing that, Imes could inject George with a sedative. He didn't like option two right now, because of the wild, frenzied way in which George conducted his necrophilia. He didn't think George would hesitate to scratch or bite him, and one missing chunk of flesh from his left arm from the late rhesus monkey Wally was one too many. That wound, inflicted while trying to quell monkey outrage and violence, had taken twelve stitches and a long time to properly heal. He still bore a dental-imprint-like scar as a reminder of his carelessness at choosing to inject Wally with the sedative.

No, this didn't warrant a sedative. Not yet anyway.

He walked briskly to a safe in a corner of the lab, used a combination to open it, and quickly pulled out a folded sheet of paper. He opened it. He should have had this code memorized by now, but with all the adjustments of late, including his to-date successful effort at preserving the life of Melvin Tierney, facilitate Velvet and Nathan's comfortable transition, it had simply slipped his mind. As he opened the paper and read, he made a mental note to keep it closer to his person—maybe inside his trusty computer tablet—along with the violence-activation code, and commit them both to memory.

"B4677C71G," he said.

George hesitated, rolling wild eyes at Imes. Then George returned his attention to Gina and began a slower and more deliberate thrust.

"Why isn't this working?" Imes said. Louder: "B4677C71G."

George stopped, looked at Imes curiously, returned his gaze to Gina, dismounted, and crawled alongside her. As he spooned the dead monkey, he let out a slow weeping, almost keening sound.

George was sad and horrified. He had killed his soulmate.

Imes extracted his computer tablet, logged the violence-quelling code into it, returned it to his pocket and approached the cage. What to do? What to do? If he told Stiessman, he would receive a stern reprimand, may even be pulled from Project Nobleman and replaced by other younger subordinates gunning for his position. The first man that came to mind was claw-faced Jeffery Laines. Imes was sure he was in cahoots with archenemy Rice Sterling. Sterling would like nothing better than to see Imes demoted, his status as top-level advisor, inventor of P-744, reduced to that of laboratory assistant, a lackey who upper echelon staff wouldn't hesitate to order to manhandle an unruly monkey and risk getting his eyes clawed out.

This was a polylemma he didn't immediately have an answer for. To do nothing would mean putting the lives of multiple test subjects at risk, not to mention national security. He imagined sending chemically-enhanced warriors—Velvet and Nathan striding confidently alongside troops—onto the battlefield and watching them, in the rising fury of battle, drop their pants and begin butt-fucking, fudge-packing and fornicating, while the enemy opened fire and slaughtered them all, laughing at the idiocy of the opposing forces the entire time. A carnival of horrors. A demented shooting gallery.

"George," he said soothingly, opening the cage. In better days George had been one of the most affectionate, intelligent and well-behaved subjects, even developing a bond with Imes, who often removed George from his prison, allowing him to wander around the lab playfully for long stretches of time while Imes worked. He would come when he was called, even hug the doctor at times. His playful antics often sparked a chorus of laughter from Imes and other staff.

George released Gina, approached the cage and held out open palms toward Imes. He squealed softly. Hug me, please. Comfort me in my time of need.

Imes opened the latch, took the monkey in his arms and held him close, smearing his white lab coat red. He carried George over to a large sink, hosed him down with warm soapy water, towel-dried him, injected him with a sedative—which George took without complaint—and placed him inside another cage out of view of Gina.

"Don't you worry, George," Imes said, patting him on the head gently as he closed the cage. "Everything's going to be okay." George looked up at Imes sadly and plunked down on his butt. Imes watched as his eyes slowly closed. George curled up into a fetal position and went to sleep.

Imes retrieved a plastic bag, donned some rubber gloves, and approached the cage containing Gina. He stuffed her in the bag, went to a nearby incinerator, opened a three-foot diameter square steel door and dropped her in. He pressed a button labeled BURN, turned the temperature to 400 degrees Fahrenheit, heard the familiar whoosh of flames exploding behind the steel door, and returned to his desk. He reached into a drawer, pulled out a black leather-bound formula book and began flipping the pages, trying to find exactly where he went wrong.

He absently pressed a button that would show simultaneous live video of Nathan and Velvet. A screen of white snow and static appeared and then he remembered. The big bomb had knocked out audio-video surveillance to parts of District 101. Sterling and his team were supposedly working around the clock to restore it. Since their arrival, he didn't have the benefit of watching or listening to the test subjects here. On the aircraft carrier yes, but not on District 101.

His cell phone beeped, startling him. He dog-eared the formula book, returned it to the drawer, and frowned as he recognized Stiessman's number. Imes wiped a furrowed brow as he answered. "Yes sir."

Stiessman's tone was impatient. "The chopper's bringing in zero-one. It's about to land. Where are you?"

Glancing at his wristwatch, Imes realized he had forgotten. He was supposed to be at the West Corridor landing pad ten minutes ago to meet Melvin Tierney. He had convinced Stiessman to stay Melvin's execution, claiming he was getting positive results with the increased dosage of P-744. For the time being at least, Melvin's insanely delusional qualities, violent outbursts and incoherent ramblings had vanished. On the surface, it seemed like a remarkable recovery. "I'm in the lab, sir. I'm on my way."

"Get your ass in gear, Doctor Imes. And you better be right about zero-one. Or it's your ass on the line."

Chapter Twelve

"There's a fine line between celebrating someone's life and mourning their death," Velvet said, sipping scotch from a plastic cup later that afternoon.

"I think if you love them, you owe them a period of mourning before celebrating their life," Nathan said, pouring another drink from the three-quarters full bottle on the coffee table. He sipped and set it down. "Like, it would be extremely disrespectful to go out and buy a new car or jump into another relationship right away after the death of a significant other."

"Really?" Velvet asked, getting up from the armchair opposite Nathan. She extended a hand and he passed her the bottle. She took it, refilled her cup, and sat in the armchair. "What about us?"

Nathan knew she was referring to their lovemaking sessions, particularly the steamy session—a short time after Cadence's murder—when they had escaped PEI by boat and ended up in an abandoned house on The Rock. "Velvet, that's different. I think we had mitigating circumstances, like surviving a post-apocalyptic nightmare, being hunted by The Neanderthals, zombie attacks, mutant animals, birds. Fuck, I'm sure I'm missing something. We were fighting for our lives. The only thing we had was us. We had no clue if we were the only people on the planet ..." Nathan trailed off.

Velvet's features darkened.

Silence.

Maybe he should never have broached the subject, he thought. It probably just brought a fresh stab of pain to a heart that surely must be still grieving over the loss of her daughter.

But, at least they had alcohol and Nathan hoped it would go some way to dulling his senses, putting a layer of intoxication over the mess that was his psyche. Imes had made good on his promise of scotch. The doctor had even gone a step further. The soldier who delivered the scotch a few hours ago had also dropped off a carton of cigarettes. So, like any good citizen trying to overcome his demons, Nathan had marched over to Velvet's house, rang her bell, and invited her over for a drink—a drink that would give them both an opportunity to challenge their violent impulses with respect to the opposite sex. Come to grips with all that love-hate shit and prove once and for all that P-744 had nothing to do with it. It was—Nathan was trying to convince himself—merely an anti-radiation drug. Plain and simple. No secret government agenda. Just an effort to help the survivors of a terrible disaster.

But, if Nathan had to be honest with himself, he still harbored some resentment toward Velvet for making that fateful decision to get the fucking picture of her deceased daughter Lisa. Maybe he had a secret agenda to extract that dagger of resentment from his heart and stab it right through the heart of Velvet Jones.

"I suppose you're right," Velvet said. "It was just sex between us anyway. I told you then and I'll tell you now, it didn't mean anything. But I'm not sure you owe anyone a period of mourning before celebrating their life. Maybe that's not what they would have wanted. Look at us on The Rock.

Part of that intimacy had to do with us wanting to celebrate Cadence's life."

There was that word again—Cadence. That word that brought so much pain. It got Nathan's back up. "What're you talking about? What the fuck do you think I was doing on that boat? In some daze, bailing out water while you steered us to safety. I was an emotional wreck. Even you told me to snap out of it, that you needed me frosty, something like that." Nathan reached for a cigarette, lit it, took a long drag and exhaled a cloud of blue-gray smoke into the air, watching as the humming air purifiers slowly sucked it out to who knew where.

"Okay, don't get your shit in a knot. I guess the point I'm trying to make—and I'm not doing a good job at it—is grieving is an individual thing. One person just might go out and buy a new car after the death of someone close, the other one may wallow in self-pity, or mourning, whatever you want to call it, for a period. Maybe the person cruising around in the new Mercedes is inwardly grieving the loss, outwardly celebrating the person's life. The fine line, grieving and celebrating at the same time. Healing. Different coping mechanisms."

"So tell me, Velvet, how were you coping when you decided to return to your house to get your daughter's photo? Were you celebrating her life, or mourning her death? Or doing both at the same time, like you said?"

Velvet's body stiffened and she set her drink down. Her hand absently moved to the front pocket of her jeans, where she still kept the tattered photo of thirteen-year-old Lisa. "Where are you going with that? What are you accusing me of?"

"Well it seems to me if you weren't so preoccupied with that photo, Cadence might be here with us right now enjoying a drink. Who knows, maybe we'd be having a threesome."

Velvet was up, across the room, and grabbing Nathan by the throat before he even had a chance for another swallow of scotch, never mind a drag on the smoke. "Do you think I killed Cadence? Is that what you think?" Velvet said, her face reddening with rage as she choked Nathan.

Nathan gasped and moved to set his drink down, but she smashed it out of his hand with a backhand slap. Then she resumed choking him. Scotch splattered the couch and coffee table while the plastic cup clattered hollowly. The cigarette in his left hand dropped and rolled along the floor. "Who ... do ... you ... think ... killed her?" Nathan said, struggling to breathe, not even trying to break the chokehold.

Anger thinned Velvet's lips. "You're a fucking asshole, you know that? A fucking asshole! You didn't even know Lisa, so don't go disgracing her memory. Who killed Cadence? Karl Mulligan killed her, that's who. That fucking savage. And you killed him, in case your sputtering memory needs to be kick-started."

"Le ... let ... me ... go pl—"

She released her grip, stepped back, staring at him with poison darts.

Nathan finally caught his breath, coughed three times and stared up at her ruefully, expecting another attack. He almost welcomed it.

She pulled the tattered photo of Lisa out and waved it in front of his face. "You would deprive me of the only good memory I have left? The only chance I had to do something good in my life was Lisa. I wanted this photo to remind me of that. Is that too much to ask? You would begrudge me that? I didn't know The Neanderthals would be waiting for us. I asked Cadence if we should go. She agreed. Do you remember?"

And as she said it, Nathan realized it was true. He suddenly did remember. They had voted on it democratically, and he had lost two to one. Cadence could have voted either way, but it was just who she was. Selflessly giving love and nurturing to others, typically without regard for her safety, well-being, or happiness. Always putting others' needs ahead of hers.

How could he blame Velvet for Cadence's death? Velvet had saved his life and rescued him from the holocaust. At least give her the decency of allowing her to honor the memory of her only child. *What the fuck is wrong with me, anyway? Is she right? Am I just a fucking asshole? Is that who I am? But sometimes I could just kill her. Fuck her to death. Shut up ... shut up, you're losing your mind.*

"I'm sorry," he said. "I haven't been myself lately."

But she was already at the door. "Fuck you, Nathan! Fuck you all to hell!" And she slammed the door so violently the small house shuddered as the metallic clang echoed eerily within the walls of his mind.

Chapter Thirteen

Closing the door to her home, Velvet had half a mind to turn around, march back to the asshole's home and kick the living shit out of him. *Or fuck the living shit out of him, whichever comes first.*

She went into her kitchen, opened the fridge, uncorked a bottle of red wine—thank God army boys deliver—and poured a drink. She went into the living room and slumped on the couch. She took a long drink, lit a cigarette, took a long drag, and puffed a cloud of smoke into the air while she absently stared out a small window at the blazing orange setting sun.

It wasn't long before her thoughts drifted back to her daughter, and how she'd mistakenly exposed Lisa to abuse at the hands of a using, abusing, sponging ex-boyfriend named Eric Saunders. Eric was much more than a joker, a smoker and a midnight toker. He was all of those things, and he was also a taker.

Big-time.

He took Velvet's pride, her self-esteem, her self-respect, her money (she could barely support them when she first hung a shingle up as a website designer, but slowly her talents were recognized and the business began to thrive) and the last thing Eric tried to take was Lisa's self-respect and self-esteem.

That had been his one big mistake.

The memory was as clear now as it was then. Eric was sitting in the living room of the house they shared, watching a hockey game on TV, drunk, while Lisa, nearby, constructed a house with Lego blocks. Unlike other girls her age, she didn't play with Barbie dolls. She had constructed a Leaning Tower of Pisa remarkably similar to the freestanding bell tower in the Italian city of Pisa.

Lisa turned to Eric with a proud smile after assembling the last block. "What do you think, Dad?"

Eric wasn't her real father. Lisa was the product of a one-night-stand with a man Velvet had met in a bar who, after finding out she was pregnant, fled.

Eric looked at the creation with distaste. "Shut your mouth, I'm trying to watch the game."

Velvet was in the kitchen cooking spaghetti when she heard him raise his voice to her daughter. When Eric first moved in with Velvet, he *had* been loving to Lisa, *had* earned enough of her respect that she called him dad. But, over the last three months, dissatisfied with his inability to find work, he had turned to the bottle. More and more his temperament had turned nasty. In one drunken binge he even threatened physical violence against Velvet. Velvet thought it was only a matter of time before he actually made good on those threats. And, she would be damned if she was willing to subject her only daughter to the same psychological scarring—not to mention physical assaults—she had suffered at the hands of her abusive father.

Spatula in hand, Velvet entered the living room and watched.

Lisa, a second time: "Don't you like it, Daddy? It's the Leaning Tower of Pizza!"

Eric's eyes blazed: "I said shut the fuck up while I'm watching the game. It's overtime." He flung his half-full beer bottle at Lisa (Velvet didn't know to this day if he was aiming for the Leaning Tower of Pisa or the Leaning Flower of Lisa; and she didn't care). The beer bottle narrowly missed Lisa's head, striking her proud creation and shattering it into a million pieces.

Velvet would never forget the hurt and fearful expression on her daughter's face. A lone tear snaked down her pudgy face, and hung on the tip of her small nose. And in that split-second, she had vowed never again to let bad judgment result in the suffering of her only child.

"Go to your room, honey," she told Lisa softly. "I'll be up in a minute."

Lisa burst into tears and sprinted up the stairs.

Velvet, meanwhile, went into the barn and returned with a sawed-off shotgun. Eric, scratching his beer belly, was staggering into the kitchen for another beer when she returned. She waited until he opened the fridge. "We're out of beer," the unemployed loser said. "Would you mind running to the store?"

She leveled the shotgun at the back of his head and cocked the hammer. "Get the fuck out of this house. Now!"

Eric had offered a token resistance at first, claiming he was sorry, he would make it up to her, all the usual bullshit. But, one swift crack to the side of the head with the stock of the shotgun told him very quickly she meant business. He called a friend, Sammy Sideman, who showed up a short time later in a pick-up truck. Sammy helped Eric pack his few personal belongings, and then they hauled ass down the driveway and off the property. Velvet, aided by a loaded shotgun, had been kind enough to supervise the eviction.

A year later, she heard through the gossip grapevine that Eric was doing time in prison after being convicted on two counts of assault causing bodily harm and one count of rape—all the violence directed at former girlfriends and in one case, even an ex's fifteen-year-old daughter.

That was then. This was now. Now, Lisa was dead, killed by radiation poisoning, so Velvet had heard.

And Eric, she had heard, had been killed at the hands of the murderous Neanderthals.

Good riddance, you fucking loser, Velvet thought, entering the kitchen, refilling her wine glass and returning to the couch. She would like to think it was as easy as blaming Eric. But she knew that wasn't entirely true. Velvet couldn't claim total victim. That would be a cop-out. She had invited the man into her house even though she could see signs of his instability from the very beginning. *Why?* she asked herself. Back then, she supposed she wasn't comfortable enough in her own skin to be by herself, a single mom raising Lisa without a male role model. The abuse she had suffered growing up had left her traumatized, a vacuum cleaner sucking up debris and dirt. She would rather be with a dirt bag than no one at all.

Gazing outside at the orange-gray sky, an understanding washed over her. She realized she was overcompensating now for the way she had been then. Now, she would rarely let anyone inside that heart. It was protected by a thick coat of impenetrable armor.

But what about Nathan? She had let him glimpse her soft side. Why? The answer shook her out of her reverie like a slap in the face. P-744. That was the reason she had accepted his invitation for a drink. She had started the conversation earlier and wanted to finish it tonight, bring him around to her way of thinking. They had been good allies in the past. She needed an ally again. She couldn't do this all on her own. Normally, Nathan wouldn't act like an asshole. It was the P-744. It wasn't him talking. It was the personality-altering drug—the same drug that was warping her better judgment and causing love-hate impulses to flare up. They had to get off P-744.

There were no more injections.

It must be in the food. The food must be spiked.

She returned to the kitchen, opened the fridge, and started removing food items and smelling them. She stopped at a plastic-wrapped bowl of green sludge. What had Imes called it? Right, total meal replacement, or TMR. She removed the plastic wrap and smelled it. There was a hint of an acrid, coppery smell, or was it more like crushed aspirin? Something unnatural, she thought. It didn't taste bad—a mixture of applesauce, steak and potatoes with a hint of horseradish—but taste could be deceiving.

She spooned out a teaspoon and globbed it on the kitchen counter. A large black fly buzzed into the kitchen, the first insect she had noticed. She stepped away from the counter as it circled her head and landed on the counter, inching its way to the green sludge. *That's it. Eat it.*

But it didn't.

She stepped back and the black fly took flight, circling her head twice—she fought an urge to swat the damn thing—before landing beside the TMR again. It inched its way toward the glob and hopped on top of it. It fed on it for a while before buzzing off again. But this time it didn't circle her head. In a wavy but deliberate trajectory, it buzzed right for the living room window, crashing into the glass and dropping to the floor with a soft click.

Inconclusive at best, Velvet thought, approaching the insect. She kneeled down and flicked it with a spoon. It slid a few inches and stopped. It was dead. Was it the TMR? She didn't know, but it was certainly suggestive. It was flying with coordination prior to ingesting TMR. But, after eating the sludge, it seemed to develop a death wish.

Chapter Fourteen

Melvin Tierney didn't think he had a death wish at all. Not anymore. In fact, he felt fine. Fine, fine, fine. He vaguely remembered escaping from his prison, searching for Larynda but encountering Sterling and the steel grip of Sterling's gun. He also recalled landing in the infirmary for a few days, suffering nasty cuts, bruises and a few lumps on his head. Severely concussed, Imes had said. He still sported a white bandage wrapped around his head, covering thirty-six stitches and two goose-eggs—until time, the great healer, could make things right again.

And right they would be, he'd thought to himself twenty minutes ago when he spotted that long black-haired beauty with the nice ass, black t-shirt, protruding nipples and beautiful mane of flowing long black hair, storm out of the house next to his, slam the door and march down the street to where she entered what was presumably her abode. It seemed Melvin had a feisty and attractive female neighbor. Sure, he had heard some arguing coming from the home next door prior to that hottie hastily exiting, but this wasn't a perfect world. It was a post-apocalyptic world.

He had chalked up the blood-filled images of Larynda as a horrible nightmare. He hadn't met her at all, Imes had assured him. She had taken ill and simply wasn't up to company. That was that. The violent visions were merely a product of a traumatized mind. Who wouldn't be traumatized surviving a nuclear bomb, bio-weapon, raging zombies and attacking mutant animals?

It was enough to make anyone stark raving mad, Melvin thought, cackling out loud between loving spoonfuls of TMR. "I like this shit," he said, wiping some green dribble from his chin, smearing it on his lips, then licking it into his mouth. "It tastes real good."

He shoveled the last spoonful into his mouth, tossed the spoon into the bowl with a clatter and watched as a black fly circled the bowl twice before landing on top of a dime-sized drop of TMR inside it. The fly ate a few morsels and flew at Melvin, bouncing off his forehead before landing on the kitchen table. Melvin pounded a fist down hard, but the fly buzzed away just in time to avoid instant death, flying straight at his head a second time. It bounced off and landed on the floor, where Melvin spotted it and squashed it with a beige Kodiak steel-toed work boot.

"That'll teach you, you aggressive little fuck," he said, wiping his mouth a second time. He entered the living room and plopped himself on the couch. It was comfortable, he thought. Imes was right—this was a damn sight better than the dungeon-like quarters he had occupied previously on that chunk of metal floating in the ocean. Before that, his memory was vague, but he seemed to remember better quarters. *Traumatized, that's all. Traumatized.*

Sure, Imes had looked a little rattled when he met him at the landing base, drove Melvin to his new home in an electric golf cart, and began outlining the recovery process of trauma. Imes didn't sound convincing when he said part of recovery from post-traumatic stress disorder was blanking out painful memories. But maybe the good doctor just had other shit on his mind. As chief physician on the ship and District 101, he must have a lot of stress and a heavy workload. Maybe that would go some way to explaining the doctor's slightly trembling hands a little later as he explained some basic house functions, and headed for the door, telling Melvin he had important business to attend to. But he promised to visit tomorrow and introduce him to the new "completely delightful" neighbors.

"Completely delightful," Melvin said, getting up and approaching the window. He watched two armed soldiers sitting in a parked green golf cart, surveying the neighborhood. They spotted Melvin in the window. He waved and smiled. So did they. After a few minutes of muted conversation—their animated expressions gave away that they were joking about something—they drove away slowly, occasionally shining a bright beam of light into windows of other residences dotting the street.

"Completely delightful," Melvin said. "My neighbors are completely delightful." He watched a tent grow in his pants and smiled, remembering the cavalier days of old when all the horny housewives on PEI wanted to fuck his brains out.

Then an ugly image flashed in his mind—Larynda. *"Fuck me four times. I want number four."*

She's naked. She wants more. Me on the bed, gouging out that loud-mouthed bitch's eyes. Screams, terrible screams. Splat. Eyeballs hit wall. More screams. Stop screaming! Punches, punches, punches—red rage. Blood, lots of blood. Finally silence. Her face, pulp, who is she now? Not a loud-mouthed bitch, that's for sure. No, no, no. A nightmare. Post-traumatic stress disorder. Just like the doc said.

It took Melvin a little time to realize he was staring out the window but only seeing the horrible images of his tortured psyche. Slowly he pushed out the horrible images and let the real world in. His handsome smile of old returned, albeit somewhat bruised from Sterling's beating.

And the throbbing in his pants decided it. "Time to meet the hottie. I couldn't hurt a fly."

*****

After showering and changing into loose-fitting black travel pants and a fresh black t-shirt, Velvet was poking at the dead fly with a spoon again when the doorbell rang. Her hair was tied back in a ponytail, still damp from the shower. She tightened, startled, realizing with a frown that her nerves were strung tighter than she'd thought. The two—or was that three?—cups of wine evidently hadn't helped much.

She peered through the window at the man in orange coveralls. *Funny,* she thought. *We're allowed civilian clothes, but he isn't. He looks familiar.* She looked at the clock on the wall: 7:46 pm. She had no idea if that represented real time or something the government had concocted since the destruction of most of the planet. But, real time or not, at least he wasn't calling at an ungodly hour. She knew it had to be Melvin Tierney, the new neighbor she had heard about. Imes had said little about the man other than he was "handsome and gentle, if a little traumatized by recent events." Yet she wasn't prepared to let her guard down.

She went to the door and pressed the intercom. "What do you want?"

"I'm Melvin, your new neighbor. I'm just being neighborly."

"What do you want?"

"Just came to say hello is all. Introduce myself."

Velvet opened the door a crack and peered at Melvin. He grinned widely. She thought it might be an attempt at seduction, but wasn't sure. Then she remembered. Melvin had showed up at her PEI acreage one day in his beat-up pick-up to remove debris. She still remembered the slogan painted in red letters on the doors: *Got Junk? Got Truck*. A poet he was not. But, yes that's it, Melvin was the town slut who would remove your junk and fuck your junk doggie-style while your spouse was away working like a dog, trying to put bread on the table.

Hadn't the dirtbag made a pass at her? Yes, he had. She still remembered his line. He had been cleaning up a slash pile of timber, chain-sawing pieces and tossing them into the truck. "I'm pretty good with my stick ... I mean sticks," he had said while taking a short break. He was drinking a glass of water she had offered him in the heat of the summer afternoon. "I've got a woody ... I mean, I'm good with wood."

Wasn't there another line just before he left? Velvet was sure there was. Something rather blunt: "You look a little stressed. Why don't I come in and help you relax? I give great oral ... I mean back massages."

She hadn't fallen for it then. But now, who knew. There were parts of her physiology she no longer felt in control of. "Don't I know you?"

"Dunno. But you can get to know me if you let me in."

She opened the door a little wider. "Got junk? Got truck? Is that you?"

Melvin raised his eyes as if peering right inside his brain for the answer. "That's me. Did I see your junk?"

"You removed ... wood debris from my property. Tried to make a pass at me. It is you. Melvin Tierney, the guy who single-handedly fucked—how many?—probably two-thirds of the women on the Island."

"Hey, I just came over to say hello. I never did anything to any woman didn't want it done to her."

Velvet felt her face redden as she pulled open the door a few more inches and sized him up. "You're an opportunistic sexual predator, nothing more. Prey on women when they're emotionally weak and vulnerable—maybe not the worst kind of human being, but definitely in the top five."

"Listen, I didn't program the DNA of women who want to cheat. I'm just there to satisfy their urges. Hell, once word got out, the phone went crazy. They came looking for me. But, if you have a problem with me, I can go ..." He turned to leave.

She didn't know why she said it. "Wait ... come in for a glass of wine."

Melvin spun around, the come-fuck-me grin returning to his boyish features. "Okay."

She led him into the living room. He sat down on the couch. She went into the kitchen and returned with a bottle of wine and a plastic cup. She poured him a drink, sat down in an armchair and picked up her half-full drink from the coffee table.

"Nice digs," Melvin said. "Exactly like mine. Let's a have a toast."

"To what?"

"How about to us becoming friends?"

"Not friends with benefits?"

"No."

"Okay ... just friends," Velvet said, standing and touching her plastic cup to his. They drank and set them down almost in unison.

"The doc says I'm recovering quite well from the trauma of our ordeal," Melvin said, his eyes darting around the house as if expecting a ghost to appear at any second. "Initially there were some gaps, terrible nightmares and stuff, but now I feel much better. How about you?"

"I don't trust much of what Imes says. He felt my distrust first-hand—a black eye."

"Oh, I think the doc is a good man," Melvin said, slurping the wine with an annoying bubbling sound. "I believe everything he says. He's only trying to help." *Melting Pot, melting pot, who's melting in the pot now?*

"Are you okay? Your eyes ... glazed over or something."

Melvin returned a faraway gaze to Velvet. "Fit as a fiddler in a cornfield." He grabbed the bottle, arching his brow.

"Go ahead," she said, standing. "I'll just be a sec. Gotta dry my hair." She went into the bathroom, stopped at the doorway and stared at Melvin for a second. He was making the loud slurping sound. "It's not a fucking Slurpee. I know you don't have any manners, but for my sake pretend, will you? Drink it like a man with some class. This isn't some seedy pub in Charlottetown where you used to hang with your cronies."

His eyes rolled up in his head as she closed the bathroom door. *He'll get over it.*

She was towel-drying her hair, thinking what a nutcase he was, when she heard glass breaking, shattering really. Then a loud cracking sound startled her. She swung around but had little time to react as Melvin burst through the door, his eyes wild, a maniacal grin on his face, holding a broken wine bottle high above his head.

She leaned forward into the vanity to avoid the attack. Melvin's left hand reached out to grab her and she swung her arm and connected with a spinning back fist to the side of his head. The forward momentum of his charge and the surprise blow sent him flying into the shower curtain.

Velvet spun around and pushed his back hard with both hands.

He knocked the shower curtain and rod down and fell into the bathtub, the white plastic wrapped around his head and body like a vinyl ghost.

"Got truck, wanna see your junk," he said, struggling to stand and thrashing his arms, slicing the plastic shower curtain with the jagged edges of the broken bottle. It pierced through the plastic and he thrust it up for a split-second like a macabre symbol of the torch of enlightenment on the Statue of Liberty.

In the bathroom, Velvet searched for a suitable weapon but found nothing. She hurried into the kitchen, grabbed a frying pan, and approached the bathroom. *Out of the frying pan into the fire. No ... knocked out with the frying pan and thrown into the fire. Better.* She cocked it like a baseball bat and slowly stepped inside the bathroom. Melvin, mumbling and muttering, was struggling to get to his feet, trying to shed his vinyl snakeskin.

Her doorbell rang.

She ran to the door, peered through the peephole, and saw Nathan standing there, awkwardly staring down at his hands. She opened the door.

"You forgot this," he said, presenting the picture of Lisa.

"Help me," Velvet said, without accepting it. She grabbed his arm, pulled him inside and closed the door.

Nathan stuffed the picture inside his pocket and looked up in time to see Melvin burst through the bathroom door and charge toward them, brandishing the broken bottle. His eyes were wide and far away, the left side of his face red and starting to swell.

Velvet swung the frying pan and narrowly missed his head. He thrust the glass toward her chest and she stepped back.

Nathan stepped into the fray and Melvin flashed him an angry look, swinging the bottle in a sweeping motion toward his throat. Nathan stepped back. Jagged glass teeth narrowly missed him.

Velvet seized the opportunity, stepping forward and ringing the frying pan off the side of his head. It clanged hollowly.

Melvin staggered back. "Fucking little cunt," he said.

Then he did something unexpected. He dropped the broken bottle, put his head down and charged like a raging bull, striking Velvet in the chest, smashing her into the wall and landing on top of her. The frying pan slipped from her hand and clattered along the floor.

As Melvin clutched Velvet's neck with both hands and began strangling her, Nathan grabbed the frying pan, approached from behind and cracked him on the back of the head hard. His bandaged head twitched slightly, but he tightened his grip on Velvet's neck, gritted his teeth, and intensified his efforts to murder her.

"Hit him again," Velvet shouted, gasping for breath.

"Let's see your junk, fucking cunt," Melvin said, his knuckles turning white with the force of the grip.

Nathan cracked the frying pan over Melvin's head one, two, three more times but it didn't deter the choking fool from his task. Nathan ran into the kitchen, replaced the flying pan with a toaster, and returned. He crammed his hand into the toast slot, ran up behind Melvin, and started smashing him over the back of the head.

Velvet's eyes bulged as her face reddened, her breath coming in short, panicked gasps as she began raking her fingernails over Melvin's face, trying to gouge his eyes out.

The sixth blow from the toaster finally loosened the attempted murderer's grip. Melvin released one hand and swung a lazy fist at Nathan, who dodged it easily and cracked Melvin over the head a seventh time. As Velvet gasped for breath, Melvin loosened the other hand and slumped over, his head thudding on the wooden floor hard, a pool of blood fanning out around him.

Nathan grabbed Melvin's arm and dragged him all the way off Velvet. She rolled over and began coughing, clutching her throat and struggling to breathe.

Nathan attended to Velvet, glancing between the dented toaster in one hand, Velvet coughing on the floor, and Melvin lying face-first, knocked unconscious from the toaster blows.

"Fucker tried to kill me," Velvet said, regaining her composure. Red handprints were visible on her neck. She stared at Melvin.

"Are you okay?" Nathan said, standing up and offering a hand. She nodded, took it. He pulled her up and helped her over to the couch.

After a few moments of silence, he extracted the picture of Lisa from his pocket and handed it to Velvet. "You forgot this. I'm sorry about what happened earlier."

"Forget about it," Velvet said, taking the picture and looking at it a long moment before tucking it in her pocket. "You saved my life. I'll forgive you."

Nathan was about to hug Velvet when an ambulance siren wailed in the distance, quickly growing louder. Two soldiers burst through the door, looked at Melvin, and then trained assault rifles on Velvet and Nathan.

Nathan threw up his arms. So did Velvet.

"He tried to kill us," Nathan said.

After a few seconds, the soldiers lowered their rifles and slung them over shoulders. They removed Melvin from the house and left. One returned a short time later, opened the door a crack, and stuck his head inside. "Are you okay?"

They nodded.

"Please stay home," the soldier said. "There'll be questions later."

He closed the door and left.

The sound of the ambulance siren grew weaker and eventually subsided, leaving Nathan sitting beside Velvet, no longer trusting himself enough to hug her, and wondering grimly how it was they had been rescued from one nightmare only to enter another potentially more terrifying nightmare. *If you can't trust your neighbors, who can you trust?*

Chapter Fifteen

"Neighbors are supposed to be friendly," Commander Stiessman snapped. His brow was wrinkled. Anger narrowed his eyes and tightened his lips. "We can't have people going around attacking people. This is supposed to be an ordered, well-behaved society."

Imes didn't know what to say. He twiddled his fingers and stared down at the little circles he was making in his hands as Stiessman tore a strip out of him. It was the following afternoon, and Imes sat across from the commander in a conference room of the administration wing. Imes knew Stiessman executed most of his orders from a control room atop a tower above the general administration buildings. But he had never set foot in it, knowing it was reserved for top brass whose rank permitted their ears to listen to classified information.

Corporal Rice Sterling, the lone soldier in attendance, stood at the door, white-knuckled fingers gripping assault rifle trigger, barely concealing a mocking grin as he watched Imes.

Imes wondered if Sterling was privy to control tower meetings.

Imes opened his mouth to speak, but the commander held up a waving finger. He shut his mouth. He was pretty sure what was coming next. "Your time with zero-one is finished."

Sterling's grin transformed into a satisfied smile as the commander continued. "I'm having Corporal Sterling execute him tonight at 1800 hours."

"Sir ... you can't do—"

Stiessman pounded a fist on the oak table with such fury it spilled water from a glass and the thumping sound reverberated within the metal walls. "Enough, Doctor Imes! I can and I will!" His eyes bored into Imes. "Do I make myself clear?"

Imes nodded meekly. "Crystal clear."

"What?"

"Crystal clear, sir."

Stiessman cleared his throat, the creases in his brow becoming less pronounced. "Now, let's discuss P-744, your brainchild, Doctor Imes. It would seem it's not the wonder drug we thought."

Imes clasped his hands together tighter, an effort to prevent them from shaking. Watching Sterling massage the trigger of the assault rifle—Imes was sure he saw Sterling wink at him—he was afraid he might well be standing alongside Melvin facing an execution squad, which he knew Sterling would not only appreciate, but relish.

"I wanted to talk to you about P-744," Imes finally said. "I need to make a few adjustments before we can proceed."

Stiessman arched his unibrow and clenched his fist. "Before we can proceed? Before we can proceed? You're telling me *now* you need to make a few adjustments before we can proceed? I think you're missing something, Doctor Imes. We *are* proceeding. We have been proceeding. We're going to drop three hundred test subjects into a mock battle in two days. If things go to plan, we're deploying them on Prince Edward Island to wipe out the last of those murdering Neanderthals, or whatever the fuck they call themselves."

Imes was leaning forward in his chair, but at Stiessman's angry tone and the F-bomb, he jerked back, as if dodging a slap in the face. He had only heard the commander swear a few times before, and each time was followed by drastic measures, such as death or demotion. *Fuck. Fucked to death.* He shuddered, wondering which one Stiessman had in store for him. One, or maybe both.

"There's a side effect I think you need to know about," Imes said.

"Are you talking about what happened to Gina?" Stiessman said. "Or zero-one?"

Imes was surprised Stiessman knew about Gina. Melvin, well, that was another story. Sterling had questioned Velvet and Nathan about Melvin's attack. A full report would have already found its way to Stiessman's eyes. But Gina? *Sterling and Laines. Those fucking assholes probably recorded it for Stiessman's benefit.* "Yes, sir. I was going to tell you about Gina."

The commander scowled. "When?"

"As soon as I determined the corrective measures. I didn't want to come to you with a problem, sir. I wanted to come to you with a solution," Imes lied.

"I'm afraid your time for solutions is up," Stiessman said, waving a hand to Sterling, whose shit-eating grin had widened with every reprimand.

Sterling opened the door and Jeffery Laines entered—nerd glasses, short brown hair and a crisp white lab coat. He looked more like a computer geek than a chemical biologist. Laines nodded perfunctorily to Imes and sat down beside Stiessman.

Stiessman continued. "I'm sorry to say, Imes, I'm relieving you of your post as chief chemical biologist and top advisor for P-744. Jeffery Laines is stepping into your place."

Laines smiled—a fuck-you-very-much smile. "I've been working on a remedy for Doctor Imes's ... ahh ... mistakes with P-744. I can fix the sexual side effects."

Imes bristled. "You don't know anything about P-744." Imes turned to Stiessman. "Sir, you can't do this. It's my baby."

"It will still be your baby, Doctor Imes. You've gotten us this far and I'm not about to dismiss you entirely. At least not yet." The unibrow arched. "But if you ever withhold information from me—like what you did with Gina—again, you'll wish you were fighting off Neanderthals on Prince Edward Island. And another thing—you will cooperate with Doctor Laines in his efforts to improve P-744. Is that clear?"

Imes nodded slowly.

Sterling cleared his throat while Laines gloated and grinned.

Stiessman glanced at Sterling briefly before continuing: "One last thing. You no longer have rank on Rice Sterling. He's been promoted to captain. You'll obey his orders with respect to test subjects. Do you have any questions?" The last sentence was delivered with the customary note of finality, signaling an end to the revolution that had usurped Imes's efforts.

Imes knew it was a rhetorical question. "No, sir." He stared at the floor, demoted and defeated.

Stiessman waved a hand. "Well, get out of here then. All of you. Show me some progress with P-744."

Imes approached the door. Sterling opened it, smiled and curtseyed as Imes walked past.

"How're you going to kill Melvin?" Imes asked Sterling.

Sterling rolled his eyes to the barrel of his AK-47 and back to Imes.

"You can't execute people like that," Imes said.

"Zero-one will receive a lethal injection," Stiessman said, standing and imposing his formidable size. "We're not barbarians."

Chapter Sixteen

Barbarians. The word echoed angrily in Commander Stiessman's mind after the others had departed. To his mind, the other half, or the other two-thirds of the population, were barbarians. Flying off in fits of jealousy over the useless emotion called love, maiming, killing, torturing, divorcing, becoming sad, becoming happy, turning a blind eye to all logic and behaving like complete imbeciles when held in the debilitating grip of emotion. All rational thought chucked out the window like some cellophane sucker wrapper. Sucker wrapper, he thought. Good simile. At least the sucker part. That's what they were, really—suckers. Getting licked, tantalized and teased with a caring and skillful tongue until the sweet taste was too small to caress. Then molars, incisors, and fangs would chomp down and crunch them to little pieces before swallowing them and leaving the rest for the nasty stomach acids to devour. Suckers. They cause tooth decay, hypertension, and diabetes. Rotten filth is what suckers really were, cleverly disguised as pleasing sweets; detestable, rotten filth, bad for the body, bad for the soul.

Stiessman remembered the very first time he was given a sucker, had become a sucker. It was a very long time ago. He was eleven years old and Baby Ruth, a cute little blonde-haired, blue-eyed girl who lived in the neighboring acreage near Sparwood, British Columbia, had told him earlier in the day to meet him at the pond in the afternoon.

She had a surprise for Randall Stiessman.

As he left the house that windy fall afternoon, Randall glanced at Helen, his mother, who was doing what she normally did Sunday afternoons: knitting pullovers, grossly misshapen and two sizes too big; mittens with oversized thumbs and little strings attached to them so when you put them on, you could thread the strings through your jacket so you wouldn't lose the mittens. Randall hated the little strings so much he always broke them off whenever Helen gave him a new pair to wear to school. Never mind the strings—the mittens themselves were embarrassing enough. The colors: bright purple, ghastly pink with little red roses, yellow, baby blue, bright red. Helen would never knit a pair of mittens in brown, black or gray, although Randall had suggested the more masculine colors a few times.

He was about to leave to meet Baby Ruth when his mother called to him. He turned and looked. She held up a purple pullover with odd-sized yellow triangles. Randall cringed looking at the creation, thinking it would hang down to his knees and look more like a dress than a turtleneck pullover. "I've just finished it," she said proudly. "It's for you." Who else could it be for? He was an only child and his father Ray adamantly refused to wear any of Helen's creations. "Why don't you put it on? It might get chilly later."

"Mom," he protested. "I'm meeting Baby Ruth. I don't want her to think I'm some kind of a baby."

"Suit yourself," she said, scrunching her small nose like she always did when she was offended. "But at least wear it for school tomorrow. You always wear that ripped black hoody. You need something bright to brighten up your life."

Well, he had found something bright in Baby Ruth. And if he hung around much longer, his little angel wouldn't be waiting at the pond that separated their properties when he arrived. "Okay, Mom, I'll wear it tomorrow. I've got to go."

His mother unscrunched her nose, offered a plastic smile, and carefully folded the pullover. She picked up a pair of half-knitted lime green mittens and returned her attention to her favorite soap opera, *As the World Turns*.

Afraid he would arrive late, Randall broke into a run as soon as he left. The sun was setting. Baby Ruth's parents were strict, not to mention his own dictatorial father. He wanted to cherish every minute with the new love of his life. More than anything, he wondered what the surprise was. During one of their hide-and-seek games, Baby Ruth had mischievously said, "If you can find me, you can fuck me." At first Randall had been disgusted at the word. His father Ray, a retired army general, claimed, "Low language is for low-brow and uneducated people. Period."

But the more he thought about it, the more he liked the idea, while maybe harboring some father-induced distaste for the actual word fuck. But he had cycled the sentence and the denotation over in his mind for the last three days, replacing the F-bomb with words and phrases like fornicate, fool around, have sex, do the old in and out, hide the salami, bury the bacon, hammer the nail, drive the wood home and yes, even make love; even though now he hated the word love. He even had two dreams about what it would be like to ... ahem ... *wham bam thank you ma'am* with Baby Ruth. In one dream he was in a pile of hay atop a barn loft. In the other, he floated in a canoe in the small pond frolicking in the sunset.

Maybe the surprise would be a little bit of show-and-tell to get them both in the mood and build their confidence and trust in one another. It had been strengthening since they first met two years ago when Baby Ruth's family purchased the fixer-upper acreage after the last neighbors, the Samsons, had, as his father had said, "ran it into the ground like the uncivilized excuse for human beings that they are."

Randall arrived at the large log beside the pond, a wind-toppled cedar that was their meeting place. Surrounded by thick brush and large trees, the pond was at the bottom of a small valley between the properties. On one side, a trail wound its way up to Baby Ruth Pearson's acreage, and another meandered through the forest to the Stiessman residence. It was peaceful and secluded. He sat down on the old cedar, the fiery sunset casting elongated spidery shadows behind trees and brush. He wasn't there long when he heard some brush rustling.

"Randy?" Baby Ruth emerged from a thick juniper bush, approaching with her hands behind her back.

Randall grinned. *Show-and-tell.* "Whatcha got there?"

"It's a surprise. You have to wait 'til I get there."

She walked purposefully to the downed tree—their loveseat, he hoped—and sat down, inching closer. Her knee touched his leg. It sent goose bumps up his spine. She was two years his senior—yes, Baby Ruth wasn't a baby anymore, even though the nickname had stuck like glue the first time he used it. She was thirteen, a teenager, and just beginning to lose some of her tomboyishness. Her hair was neatly tied back in a ponytail and her blue eyes glimmered in the sunset. In fact, Randall was sure she had eyeliner accentuating her eyes, which would be a first for Baby Ruth. His hopes rose. *She's going to seduce me.*

He grew impatient. "I'm dying, Baby Ruth. What's the surprise?"

She put her hand on his leg and spontaneously kissed him on the cheek. More goosebumps. More excitement. More nervous tension.

"Was that it?" he asked, trying but failing to speak nonchalantly.

"No." The mischievous grin returned. She had a splash of pink blush on each cheek, but Randall didn't think that was make-up. "I just felt like doing it. Now close your eyes."

He did.

"Now open your mouth."

He did.

"Now stick your tongue out."

He complied.

He heard a sound, like the fake crackling of flames you might hear on an old 50s radio drama while a sound-effects woman in the studio crumples plastic wrap into a microphone. Then taste: sweet and sour—honey and lemon, with a hint of strawberry. He licked and smiled. "It's candy."

"It's a sucker," she said. "A lollipop. You can open your eyes."

Opening his eyes, he took the sucker in his hand and tried unsuccessfully to stuff the whole red and yellow and white candy circle on a stick into his mouth. But it was too big and round.

Ruth giggled. "You'll never get it all in, silly boy."

He withdrew it, grinning. He put a hand on her leg. She didn't object. "Thank you, Baby Ruth. Thanks for the sucker. I love it."

He moved in for the second kiss, this time aiming for the lips.

She held up a hand. "Wait. I have another surprise."

He kissed the palm of her hand, running his tongue sloppily up its length.

"Yuck," she said, jerking it away and wiping it on her blue jeans. "It's sticky."

They both giggled.

"Lick it. It's sweet. What's the other surprise?" Randall asked.

"It's Charlie."

The words were a blow. "Who?"

Randall spun around as a twig snapped in the trees nearby. A fat boy with a shock of brown curly hair, pudgy cheeks and denim bib overalls stepped out. "I heard you guys kissing," he said.

"What in the frick is this?" Randall said, standing up abruptly. He had liked the first surprise and what he thought accompanied it, but *this* was something different—something intrusive to his private time with Baby Ruth. And he couldn't help the pangs of jealousy that knotted his stomach, couldn't help regarding Charlie coldly, couldn't help, even though Baby Ruth introduced him as a new friend—"the three amigos"—the tears welling up in his eyes, couldn't even help clenching his fists and grinding his teeth as the boy extended a pudgy hand. Instead of taking the hand—he had to battle inner demons to stop himself from punching the new kid on the block—he stormed off angrily, chucking his sucker into the pond and yelling, "Don't give me any more goddamned surprises."

And that turned out to be the last thing he said to her.

A silent, sulking and sobbing week went by. Although Baby Ruth called on him three times during that week, his father Ray, a willing and encouraging accomplice in mission-ditch-Baby-Ruth, always told her the same thing: "Randall's busy and can't see you right now."

Then one day, Randall started having second thoughts about his stubbornness and unwillingness to see her. He stealthily went down to the pond, hid behind a tree, and watched and waited. He was hoping to make amends, maybe even apologize for his irrational behavior. But the scene he saw cemented his jealousy, cemented his hatred for the word love, solidified his resolve to become disciplined, ordered and unloving to the opposite sex. But oh, there was always success. He could define his strength, his manhood, by his military success. And he had succeeded beyond his wildest expectations, controlling people, controlling his emotions, calling the shots.

The scene with Baby Ruth still haunted his psyche, although he had done his father proud. He still remembered her as she was, sitting on the same log on the same spot. With him. With Charlie.

And he watched the fat slob who reminded him so much of Charlie Brown go in for that first kiss after a few moments of small talk. That first kiss—on the lips—the intimacy that was meant for Randall. And Charlie's wandering hands were roaming in places that Randall viewed as his property, his territory, his human landscape to joyfully discover.

Many years later, he learned Baby Ruth had married Charlie and was living the dream with a white picket fence, a small child and another baby in the bucket.

His father had reinforced the rift: "Women distract you from your goals and ambitions. They aren't worth taking seriously. You'll make a far better human being serving the interests of national security." Then Ray punctuated his words to live by, as he so often did, with "Period!"

Love. Such a stupid emotion, Stiessman thought. All it does is leave you silly and vulnerable. A base barbarian.

Lost in reverie, he hadn't noticed the red light flashing on a wall monitor. But when dancing colors transformed into the prim, proper and meticulously shaved face of Prime Minister Eliot Masterson, Stiessman did take notice. He checked his wristwatch. The prime minister was punctual to the second as usual.

"Commander Stiessman," the honorable Eliot Masterson said, "are you daydreaming?"

"No, Mr. Prime Minister."

"You have your report?"

Stiessman cleared his throat. "I do, sir. The P-744 ongoing trials are still going well with most subjects."

"Most subjects?"

"Well, one of the side effects—has to do with the love profile of the drug—tends to be a little extreme in some cases. I don't know how to put this politically corr—"

"Forget political correctness, Stiessman. This country, the whole world, is on the brink of total ruin and you're trying to be politically correct. Tell me the problem and tell me the solution. And make it quick. I don't have much time."

Stiessman stared at his hands, concentrating hard to avoid balling his fists. He hated being reprimanded almost as much as he hated the word love, particularly by people he viewed as intellectually inferior to himself. *The whole world is on the brink of total ruin because you and the Americans brought it there.* But he didn't bother saying it. That might come later, providing *his* secret agenda went to the letter. For now, he had to bite his tongue and serve up the rhetoric those who thought they were in control had come to rely on from Stiessman; making decisions that got the job done, never mind minor details or collateral damage. The less they knew, the easier it would be to hang him out to dry like a rotting scarecrow, should things suddenly take a turn for the worse.

He chose his words carefully. "Prime Minister, we have some sexual deviant behavior that seems to be isolated to subjects with blood type A. These subjects are starting to demonstrate an overwhelming desire to copulate frequently and for long periods of time; so long, in fact, that they risk their health or the health of their partners. One of our male lab monkeys recently fornicated with another female test subject so long and hard that she expired."

"Are you saying he fucked her to death?"

"That's exactly what I'm saying, sir. We've isolated test subject zero-one for the same reason. His sexual urges occur frequently and are accompanied by extreme violent tendencies. There was an incident with test subject zero-two and—"

"Spare me the details. I trust you're dealing with this deviant behavior."

"Yes, sir. And the solution is the talented Doctor Jeffery Laines. He's been working closely with Doctor Imes on a modified version of P-744, a version we're convinced will not react negatively with compromised blood type subjects. We're injecting specific rhesus monkeys now with the new profile."

"What about the training exercise?"

"On schedule, sir. Friday at 1600 hours. In the meantime, we're isolating and containing subjects with adverse reactions—they will not participate in the training exercise until we know the new profile will correct the disorder."

"Will these troops be ready to deploy in a week?"

"I'll see to it, sir."

"Good." There was a moment's pause while the prime minister, a 50ish man with chiseled features, thick gray-black hair, cut short and slicked back, regarded Stiessman with cold blue eyes that seemed to pierce right through him.

Stiessman offered a plastic smile and furrowed his unibrow.

Finally, the leader of Canada spoke: "What about this Doctor Imes? Were your instincts about him correct?"

"Yes. He's been subordinated to Captain Sterling and Doctor Laines. But he's agreed to carry on working for the cause."

"I don't imagine he was too happy about it."

"No, sir. But it was necessary."

"Keep me posted, Commander Stiessman. And keep an eye on Imes. We don't want him blowing the whistle on any of this."

"I will, sir."

"Good work."

The blinking red light beside it and the screen faded rapidly to black before Stiessman had a chance to say more. It didn't matter. He had other things on his mind right now. One was world domination once he got control of the genetically modified warriors; the other, and right now a priority, was the domination of one very lovely and very blonde Marilyn Buxton.

Locking the conference room door, he walked briskly down the hallway, lit hospital-like by rows and rows of fluorescent ceiling lights. He turned right, walked down another corridor, and took an elevator to his penthouse suite, one floor above the control tower where he masterminded most of his plans.

Inside his suite, he closed and locked the door, and set his communication devices to vibrate—more than that would be vibrating soon enough. He pulled off his military jacket adorned with several medals, went to the fridge, extracted a bottle of wine, plopped it into a bucket of ice and, like clockwork, received a text message on his private and untraceable phone from Captain Sterling: *Test subject 01 is scheduled for departure. Test subject 069 is scheduled for arrival in two minutes.*

Stiessman clicked a remote and the powerful, evocative music of Beethoven's fifth symphony poured into the room. He allowed himself a minute to take in the 360-degree view of District 101, inhaling with pride as he loosened his tie, unbuttoned the top three buttons of his shirt, and settled into the plush leather couch. He pressed another button and navy blue blinds lowered, obscuring the view of his command. Two orange lamps flickered to life, providing just the right ambiance. Stiessman wanted the pretense of romance even though his relationship with Marilyn, the only subject he allowed himself to think of or refer to by first name, was anything but.

During a routine inspection of P-744 trials, he had met the twenty-five-year-old former stripper. The first time he saw her through the one-way glass of an experimental chamber, she was buck-naked, humping a bedpost and moaning with pleasure, her buxom breasts flopping in rhythm to her spasmodic gyrations. Suddenly she stopped, flashed a perfect set of pearly whites and winked at the monitor, looking directly at Commander Stiessman. Responding to P-744, Marilyn liked it hard, fast, and often, displaying none of the violence blood type A subjects had shown. She was blood type B.

And there was something else. Her smile, that mischievous way she tilted her pouty lips, reminded Stiessman of Baby Ruth. With Marilyn, he thought he could somehow capture what he had lost—at least the carnal part of it—with Baby Ruth. So he had made a special arrangement with Sterling to book periodic private "interview" sessions at his penthouse. The first time he had made love with her, Stiessman had to admit she almost killed him. At sixty-four, even though he kept himself in fine shape, he was hardly able to keep up with a young nymphomaniac. But it was also intensely pleasurable and akin to what he thought Baby Ruth would be like. And with the activation and deactivation code words, he could—like using a TV remote control—turn her on and off in an instant. Even without the code words, she seemed to have a thing for Stiessman, although he was quite content to turn her on when required and turn her off when no longer required.

Even mute her if he had to. The perfect soulmate and lover, one who could not disobey or hurt him. Always there and always ready when he needed her.

He sighed. This P-744 may turn out to be better than anyone imagined. Wouldn't John Lennon be happy if he knew the government was creating a generation of lovers?

There was a chime and Stiessman went to the door. He opened it. Marilyn was dressed in a long, flowing white gown as per the commander's orders. Large breasts with erect nipples protruded almost through the sheer fabric. She winked at the commander.

Two armed soldiers stood behind her. "Here she is, sir," one said, unable to conceal a wry grin.

Stiessman didn't care. These underlings wouldn't dare undermine his authority. His reputation preceded him. They knew to speak out would mean a punishment and demotion that would blackball their military careers for life. It was nice to be powerful. Nice to be feared.

He dismissed the soldiers, let her in, and closed the door. She hugged him immediately and planted a wet kiss on his lips. Maybe he wouldn't need the activation code today. "Is my Randy randy again?" she asked, tonguing his ear.

"Yes."

She released him. "Do you have a drink?"

He went to the bar, poured two glasses of red wine and returned, handing one to Marilyn. They clinked glasses and drank.

"Do you mind if I call you Baby Ruth?" Stiessman said as Marilyn set her glass on a coffee table, pulling her dress down to reveal naked, heaving, ready breasts.

"You can call me anything you want," she said, striking a Marilyn Monroe pose on the couch. "Just don't call me late for dinner."

Chapter Seventeen

Don't be late. It's a meeting you won't want to miss. Pieces of Nathan's mind—distant memories—were beginning to flood back in as disconnected images. In the privacy of his dwelling, he sat on the couch the following evening and tried to assemble the jigsaw puzzle with so many jagged and ill-fitting pieces. It was the evening after the drama with Velvet and Melvin, and he was a little out of sorts about a few things. He had black-purple bruises on his knees and forearms, and was sure they didn't occur from the altercation with Melvin. *If not there, then where?* And his mind kept repeating *don't be late. It's a meeting you won't want to miss.*

An image of a tall, authoritarian-looking man gave the words meaning. A piece of the jigsaw puzzle fit neatly into place. *Press bashing.* The words had come from PEI district school superintendent David Dittle. As a reporter, Nathan had covered a school board meeting in the town of Montague, where many outraged parents had voiced concern over the quality of education their children were receiving in the public school system. He couldn't remember all the details, but it had something to do with cutbacks, permanent full-time teachers getting precipitously laid-off just prior to receiving full benefits and a guaranteed retirement pension, and being replaced by temps. He was in a school auditorium and a panel of school board members, led by the booming and assertive voice of Dittle, tried to defend the cutbacks, claiming the measures wouldn't affect the fine educational standards in the school district.

But some of the parents weren't convinced. One angry mother stood up, waving a fist, interrupting Dittle's monologue, claiming, "My son used to have homework, and now he says he has time to do it during class. What the hell are the temps doing in class that my son can do his homework? I'll tell you, the quality of education is going to hell."

Other parents had also voiced strong opposition to the cutbacks, some slamming the "new standard of education around here" and storming out of the meeting before it had ended. Dittle ended up red-faced and pleading with many "to stay and hear what I have to say." Nathan had convinced his editor it was groundbreaking news and Lance Symington must have believed him. That Friday's newspaper ran Nathan's story front page: *Angry Parents Oppose School Board Cutbacks.* His lead: *Angry parents lashed out at school board officials Monday, many claiming recent budget cutbacks are lowering the standard of education.*

If the parents had been angry at the meeting, some of the phone calls after the story broke were even angrier. Waving a newspaper, a disgruntled father had even stormed into Nathan's office, shouting, "You're nothing but a sensationalist hack. You should be working for *The National Enquirer.*" Then he tore the newspaper to shreds, calling it "a rag with nothing but vaudeville-style journalism," threw the pieces into Nathan's face, stormed out of the office and slammed the door so hard the office shook like a point-three earthquake.

Nathan had a hunch there would be more nasty calls, even from school board officials. And there were.

A week later, after the phone had quieted, superintendent Dittle did call. *Press bashing.* Nathan should have seen it coming. Dittle told Nathan about an "upcoming meeting in which the school board plans to fully explain how exemplary the standard of education really is."

Nathan's news for nose smelled a legitimate story. But when he went to the meeting, it was more like an illegitimate press bashing. In attendance were a select group of sympathizing school board officials and an exclusive group of parent sympathizers, apparently in denial about their children's suffering education.

Nathan's gut feeling—the one that kept saying *No, no, no … it's a set-up*—went unheeded. Sitting in a crowded gymnasium, Dittle stepped to the podium, took the mic and extolled the virtues of the high standard of education for more than ten minutes. Then the content and tone of his speech changed: "There is a reporter in the audience who has written a news story slamming the standard of education in this school district."

Nathan felt his face get hot as a blush climbed up his neck. The superintendent continued: "I'm not going to name the reporter, but he knows who he is."

Accusatory eyes scowled at Nathan. He shrank in his seat, stopped scribbling notes on his steno-pad, and stared at Dittle in shock.

Dittle's voice sharpened, his attack becoming more direct and threatening: "And I'll say this much—if this is what constitutes credible reporting here, maybe it's time we found ourselves some better journalists." He pulled out the newspaper, waving it around angrily, pointing to the headline. "This is nothing but sensationalist crap. If this reporter continues his slander and defamation of the school board, he should understand there will be serious legal ramifications."

At that, Nathan sprang up and ran out of the gymnasium. He could feel the daggers on his back as he left, feel the hatred, feel the scorn. At that moment, he had been so frightened, he thought the angry mob was going to haul ass out of the building, tar and feather, then stone him and burn him at the stake like the witches of Salem.

Driving home that evening, shaking like a windswept weeping willow, it was all he could do to keep his vehicle from careening off into a ditch. He uttered profanities and pounded his fists on the dashboard at one stop sign until an impatient motorist leaned on the horn.

Arriving home, a lone tear dripped down his cheek. He had hugged Cadence tightly on his arrival. It was her soothing words, caresses and tender loving care that had slowly helped him heal. He had initially been tempted to write another piece, tell it like it was, how an unsuspecting, honest journalist had been baited and trapped by some do-gooding school board sympathizers, school board officials and teachers who were afraid of the ugly truth and would rather wipe it under the carpet—or wipe the reporter under the carpet—and bury it forever.

But it was Cadence, the reasoned legal mind that processed information so damned logically, who had convinced him otherwise—let dead dogs lie. It wasn't like it was a groundbreaking story that would quickly gain national or international attention, she had been quick to point out. "Nobody cares. It's a small town. They want to keep it happy and peaceful. You'll just make enemies, maybe even get sued."

Thinking about it now, and he wasn't sure why he was, he realized people in the small community didn't like hearing the truth about the diminishing standard of education. A double-standard. They didn't mind attacking school board officials, but it was quite another thing to have their neighbors, with *their* kids in private schools, learn about the problem.

One big fucking competition to keep up with the Joneses. One monumental pile of bullshit. Get the golden shovel out and start scooping. It's going to be a while before you make a dent in this mountain-sized pile of dung.

Nathan absently scratched his head, stood up, and approached the window. A thick, rolling blanket of gray-black clouds covered the dome, a single orange shaft of light from the setting sun poking through a small hole in the threatening mass. Errors in judgment, he thought. He had made a few as a reporter. Like when he splashed the name of a local cop who had been unceremoniously fired on the front page of the weekly paper. After that, all his cop connections had dried up post-haste. A call to the district supervisor had changed all that—the power of the press—but relations were never quite the same. Sure, they would give him information on car accidents, sometimes even murder investigations, but never more than what they had to. Tight-lipped was too kind a phrase. Severely strained was a little better.

Maybe his journalism career had been nothing more than a comedy of errors. Black comedy, to be sure, he thought, staring at the ominous sky. Thunder boomed and white lightning cracked, sizzled and snaked down, snapping angrily mere meters from the glass dome.

Startled, Nathan jumped back from the window. *A glass menagerie. I live in a fucking glass menagerie.*

The doorbell rang.

He tightened. Then he remembered. *Right. Velvet. She wants to talk.*

He walked to the door, opened it, and stared at her blankly for a few seconds.

"You look like you've seen a ghost," she said.

"More like a press bashing mob," Nathan said. "My journalism career."

She had a harried expression. "Tell me about it another time. Let's go."

"Go? Where?"

"They've got Melvin."

"I know. He tried to kill us."

"But they're going to kill him. We can't let that happen."

"Velvet, please. We're fighting an army."

"I don't care. I'm not turning into a fucking automaton. I'd rather fight The Neanderthals. At least there I had my freedom. I knew what I was getting into. Here, we're like caged animals with no idea of what's coming next. We're not ourselves, Nathan. Haven't been for a long time." She stepped inside, grabbing his wrist. "Let's go."

"Give me a second."

She released his arm. He searched in a closet, located a black jacket and a black baseball cap—may as well match up with Velvet, he thought, whose sleek black tights and tight-fitting long-sleeved black top made her look like an angry ninja.

He changed clothes and they left.

A block later, he saw it. A green electric car, *Canadian Army* painted in white on its doors, plugged into an outlet outside a military personnel building. Through lit windows, they could see and hear soldiers cavorting and drinking inside the building.

Velvet unplugged the car, climbed in the driver seat and turned it on. Headlights illuminated and it whirred to life, the soldiers none the wiser. "Hop in. I want to show you something. I think you'll find it interesting."

Nathan climbed in and they sped down the tiny army-barracks-lined street.

Or terrifying, he thought as bowling balls of thunder rolled, sheeting rain hissed, lightning crackled, and sirens began to wail.

Chapter Eighteen

Melvin Tierney heard the sirens wail and feared the worst. "Fire," he shouted, remembering the blazing infernos that had decimated most of humanity. He jerked in the chair, but Captain Rice Sterling put a firm hand on his shoulder and pushed him back down. Not that he could have gone far. Wrapped in a straitjacket, confined in a similar dungeon-like room where he had previously made feces angels, he didn't have a lot of options.

"Hold up, cowboy," Sterling said, lowering a scowling face to within inches of Melvin's. "That's just a drill. But this isn't. Life's a journey, my friend. And you've reached the end."

"No," Melvin pleaded, white-faced and wide-eyed. His forehead glistened with crawling beads of sweat. "I didn't do anything. You guys, all the drugs. Not my fault." He jerked again and Sterling placed two hands on his shoulders, stuffing him firmly back into the chair.

"Whoa, pardner," Sterling said, gesturing with a hand to Jeffery Laines, who, wearing a white lab coat and signature black-framed nerd glasses, stood patiently over a metal table with a display of syringes arranged neatly on a white paper placemat. A shiny green plastic nametag pinned to his chest denoted his new authority: *Chief Chemical Biologist,* or a modifier and controller of human behavior in this case. With the new title, his authority was far-reaching.

Laines picked up a syringe and stepped forward.

Veins bulged in Melvin's moist neck. He twisted and squirmed in the chair.

Sterling punched him in the mouth, hard. Melvin's head snapped back, blood spraying from a cut lip.

Laines said, "You don't have to go that fa—"

"Fuck I don't," Sterling snapped. He touched a hand to his sidearm "You're standing there like Doctor fucking Kevorkian with a syringe of death, and I can't punch this loser in the face? Something wrong with that, ya ask me."

"Who's asking you?" Laines said, knowing that Sterling probably didn't outrank him, at least concerning the care and fate of test subjects. They were supposed to work together, but nowhere in the rulebooks did it say an army captain outranked a chief chemical biologist. It was a gray area yet to be addressed by legalese-worded policy and procedures manuals; a gray area that Laines could use to his advantage. If he had to. "I think we need to have a little talk."

Sterling turned away from Melvin, approached the door, unlocked it and curled a finger at Laines, who slid a metal tray table to a corner and followed. Turning to Melvin, he said: "Don't worry, he doesn't know what he's talking about. We're not going to kill you. Just sedate you."

Melvin nodded hopefully. But his eyes were wide with terror.

Laines left, locking the door behind him.

In the hall, Sterling took a little while to calm down. "Sorry," he said. "I guess it's my anger at Imes getting the better of me. You know Imes killed my wife."

Laines had heard the story more than once. He nodded sympathetically. It was Laines's sympathy for Sterling's loss that helped forge the unlikely alliance with a goal to usurp Imes and his authority. The plan had gone off without a hitch. It had been Laines who had sabotaged Imes's trials with P-744, tainting the drug with a deadly combination that had caused lab monkey George to fuck Gina to death and Melvin to kill one woman and almost kill another. Imes's reputation had been destroyed. Now, Laines could get the glory for the new and improved P-744, and Sterling could exact vengeance on Doctor Imes. But first they had to get along. And the new promotions had pushed them into a power struggle at a time when they needed each other to complete their agendas.

"Listen," Laines finally said, after they had stared each other down for a few moments. "I've got an idea. The training battle is tomorrow. Why don't we put Melvin in there?"

A thick vein on Sterling's forehead pulsated, writhing like an angry snake. His eyes narrowed "How we gonna do that?"

"One of those syringes contains a memory-loss drug that also makes subjects higher than a kite," Laines explained. "Everything becomes a surreal dream state. Inject Melvin with it and throw him to the wolves."

A pause. Sterling scratched the pulsating vein and thought. "Good idea," he said with a satisfied grin. "How many of those syringes do you have in there?"

"Two," Laines said, opening the door.

The birth of a new plan. Sterling got Imes on the phone: "Imes, I need you to come and oversee this injection immediately." He hung up without waiting for a response. He knew Imes would be too petrified not to comply with a direct order. He rubbed his hands together as he followed Laines into the death chamber. He looked at a wide-eyed and tied Melvin. He softened his tone. "Listen, Melvin. That stuff earlier. Uh ... sorry. My temper gets the better of me sometimes."

"Tell me about it," Melvin said. "You put me in the infirmary last time."

Laines wheeled the metal table with syringes close to Melvin.

"I know. I apologize," Sterling said. "As Doctor Laines said, we're just going to sedate you. I was just messing with you."

"Well, don't mess with me anymore," Melvin said, cheered a little.

Laines rolled up Melvin's sleeve, wrapped a rubber tube below the elbow, and flicked a vein in Melvin's forearm. It began to grow. He picked up a syringe, pulled the cap off the needle, squirted a few drops of clear liquid into the air and lowered it to the pulsating vein. "Just relax, Melvin. Just a little prick."

Chapter Nineteen

"Get your hand off me," Velvet said, swinging the electric vehicle around a corner that led out of the residential zone and onto a picturesque rural country road, but one that was glass-protected from what was turning into a violent storm. "Don't think with your little prick."

Nathan removed his hand from her leg. *Sex, sex, I want so much sex. I'm addicted to orgasms. Isn't everybody addicted to orgasms?* "Don't you mean little head? Otherwise I'm just a big prick."

"Maybe you are," she said with a small grin. "You said it."

Nathan ignored the comment for the time being. There would be time enough to play later, he hoped. He looked back and realized they weren't being followed. Whatever the wailing siren meant, it didn't appear to mean their vehicle theft had been noticed and they were being pursued. The sound grew fainter as they sped along the two-lane rural road. "Where are you taking me, anyway?" he asked.

"I want you to see something, so you'll believe me."

"See what?"

"It's not a what."

"Then who?"

"Don't worry, one picture's worth a thousand words. And believe me, this one speaks volumes."

Nathan decided to keep quiet and let the picture speak volumes. For ten minutes they were alone with their thoughts, until finally, up in the distance, he saw a dark gray mass of buildings to the left, lit up at four points with towers of light.

It was surrounded by a barbed-wire fence. In the middle, there was another tower, a guard station offering a 360-degree view of the compound below. Even from the distance, Nathan could see black dots moving in the square yellow windows of the circular watchtower. Guards. Armed guards, watching, waiting, ready to shoot to kill.

About three city blocks before the compound, Velvet steered the vehicle onto a winding, bumpy dirt road. Nathan ducked branches and brush clawing the vehicle—open to the elements except for the windshield—as she navigated what looked more like a bike path than a serviceable road. She pulled to an abrupt stop about a hundred yards from the ocean and climbed out.

Nathan stepped from the vehicle, noticing gigantic incoming waves in the distance, lashing violently at the protective glass dome. He shuddered, wondering grimly how much of Mother Nature's temper it could withstand before shattering completely.

Velvet ignored the sound and the fury of Mother Nature—booming thunder, crackling lightning, hissing rain and splashing waves—and pointed to a small opening in the thick brush. "Over here."

They slowly made their way through the forest, pushing away snapping, cracking, attacking branches. It was pitch black and they were guided only by the small beam from a flashlight Velvet had produced.

They arrived at the perimeter fence. She pointed. "Down there, see that hole?"

Nathan nodded, clasping his hands together in an unsuccessful effort to stop them from trembling.

"We crawl under it," Velvet said. "But be careful. The fence is electrified."

Before he could respond, Velvet started crawling into the black hole, the odd grunt escaping her lips.

Nathan stood watching.

She emerged out the other side, trained the beam on him and whispered, "Come on. What're you waiting for?"

"Velvet," Nathan whispered. "This compound is heavily guarded. We could get shot."

"There's a blind side. And this is it. Besides, this is shift change. We have a small window. Hurry."

Nathan's frayed nerves were starting to get the better of him, tentacles of fear poking at his chest, back and neck like acupuncture needles. "Tell me, what're we going to see?"

"This is where they take the deviants. The ones that don't respond well to P-744. Blood type A, I think. This is where you'll see humanity at its lowest form."

Nathan summoned dwindling courage reserves and began crawling through the hole. His jacket snagged on a sharp protruding piece of fence metal. A spark burst from the fence and he froze. He could smell burning clothes and the sweet smell of singed flesh.

"Keep going," Velvet said.

"My jacket's snagged."

"It'll tear, keep going."

He inched along, stretching the fabric. It tore. The jacket burst into flames. He scrambled out of the hole and started rolling on the ground.

Velvet knelt down beside him, quickly patting out the flames. By the time she had them extinguished, she lay on top of Nathan, her arms wrapped tightly around him. She slowly raised a black sooty hand.

In the glow of the perimeter lights, Nathan examined her hand. "You okay?"

"I burned it, but not badly. How about you ... do you feel all right?"

"A little sizzle on the back, but it's not well done."

"Medium-rare, maybe?"

"Yeah."

"We've got to start meeting like this," Nathan said.

Velvet couldn't help a small smile. "It's *stop* meeting like this, bonehead." She stood up, pointing to the jacket, now sleeveless, shredded and burned. "Get rid of that. It's toast."

Nathan stood and she peeled it off. He winced a few times, threw in a few "ow"s for good measure, and examined it as she held it up. Half the fabric on the back had also burned away in the human barbeque.

She tossed it on the ground. "Turn around."

He did.

"Your t-shirt's a little burned, but not like the jacket. Some red marks on your back. You'll live." She wiped her hand on her pants and pointed to a black manhole cover about fifty feet away. They were partially concealed from the control tower by neat rows of steel containers. "Let's go."

They ran to the manhole cover and stopped. Velvet knelt down and started twisting a large circular metal wheel attached to it. "Give me a hand."

Nathan knelt down, helping. "You've been here before?"

She nodded as they strained, finally loosening the wheel. Velvet spun it easily now. It stopped and she lifted it up. A suffused gray light lit the shaft as it curled its way underground. "I've been here before."

"What is it?"

"An airshaft, I think. Let's go."

Metal rungs—a maintenance ladder—were welded to the sides of the shaft, and Velvet began climbing down.

Nathan followed, pulling the metal door closed behind them. It clanged shut, reverberating and echoing eerily through the metal tunnel, roaring thunder from above punctuating the repetitive metallic sound.

Disconnected thoughts assaulted Nathan's mind as they descended. *Press bashing. Ed. Velvet. Dead. Time to play ... time to play later.*

Thirteen minutes later, they arrived at a fork in the tunnel, one leg extending straight down while another circled sharply right. They stopped a moment. Nathan was surprised he was hardly breathing. He was getting stronger, even though exercise had been absent from his daily regime.

Velvet noticed the recognition in his eyes. "Genetic enhancement. You're stronger and more physically fit than before. Better oxygenation of your blood, quicker muscle regeneration. Your mind's supposed to be sharper too, but in your case I'm not sure it's working. But you're enhanced. How do you like it?"

"The jury's still out. Which way?"

"Through here," she said, pointing to the curving shaft. "I don't know where the other one goes."

They continued their progress in silence. The rungs had disappeared, replaced by a silvery soft lining. Gray lights, installed at fifty-foot intervals, marked their progress. After five minutes, Nathan asked: "How lo—"

But he didn't have to complete the question. A strange cacophony of sound announced they had arrived, echoing from just ahead and below. The dissonant sounds were a frightening mixture; the carnal sounds of pleasure—"oohs" and "aahs" and "oh baby"—an orgiastic frenzy; the horrifying screams of the damned, pained sobbing and groaning, all wrapped not-so-neatly into one ear-splittingly terrifying and prolonged blast. A babel so disturbing Nathan stopped and put his hands to his ears, wincing, closing his eyes and grinding his teeth. *No, please God, no. Hell ... hell on Earth. Get me outta here. Pleeease!*

Velvet grabbed his wrist firmly. Nathan opened his eyes, unable to remove hands from ears. "Snap out of it!" she shouted.

It was more reading her lips than actually hearing the words. He could see the nervous tension etched in her face, large creases in her forehead that would probably never be erased, even with muscle and tissue regeneration from modern bio-chemical engineering.

Velvet pulled one of Nathan's hands away. "I've never heard it this bad," she said. "Something's changed."

She crawled ahead of Nathan and stopped at a metal grate. Spears of light poked in from below. She stared for a few seconds, eyes widening in horror, then waved Nathan forward. Reluctantly, he removed hands from ears, crawled forward slowly, heart thumping wildly in his chest, and grimaced at the carnage he saw below. He choked back and swallowed an acidic puke ball crawling up his esophagus, trying to make sense of the multiple violent, lust-filled scenes.

Through holes in the vent, he could make out a long corridor lined on either side by numerous steel-barred cells. In one cell, a beefy man growled, groaned and shrieked with pleasure as a man behind pounded him up the ass doggie-style. In another cell, a red-haired woman licked and voraciously slurped a man's erect penis like it was the last lollipop, the last sucker on Earth. In yet another scene, unfolding right below them in the hallway, a black-haired soldier in green battle fatigues licked a moaning woman's gaping pussy like it was a ripe and juicy watermelon. Her ample breasts bounced and heaved as she moaned with pleasure.

A few feet away, a bony elderly man was curled up in a fetal position moaning and groaning for his life. Two soldiers kicked him repeatedly in the face with black steel-toed boots, blood squirting everywhere from a head that now resembled mashed potatoes topped with salsa. He didn't have long to live.

In still another cell, a soldier stood with a firehouse trained on a young naked woman, blasting the helpless victim in the face with powerful jets of water. The woman was pinned in a corner, the pulsating liquid force pounding her head repeatedly against a concrete wall, her mouth agape and red tongue dangling out like a rabid dog. It slithered back and forth, up and down, with the force of the water in a macabre harmony with her pounding head.

Through the length of the corridor, more shouts of pain and pleasure echoed frighteningly. Whatever control the government might have exerted over this house of horrors in the past was just that—a thing of the past.

The woman lying on her back receiving cunnilingus shuddered with a powerful orgasm, shrieking with pleasure, opening her eyes wide and staring straight into Nathan's horrified eyes.

The bony, mashed-faced man uttered a final groan and went limp, the soldiers delivering four more kicks to his head just to be sure.

Nathan felt the lurching of his stomach before he realized what was happening. The puke ball that had been forced into the pit of his stomach earlier had amassed a green and yellow liquid army and issued the charge. Projectile vomit stormed up and sprayed out through the metal-screened vent, splashing onto shuddering orgasmic woman's face, on the head of cunnilingus man, onto the blood-and-brain-matter-soaked boots of the murdering soldiers.

Other bits of vomit bounced off the metal grate, spraying Nathan and Velvet in the face, chest and head.

Velvet wiped puke from her face and tugged Nathan's arm, her expression tight with fear.

The orgasmic woman sighed, pointing a trembling finger straight up at Nathan. With intently focused eyes, three soldiers followed her index finger to the vomit slinger. "We have company," she announced gleefully. "Would you like to join us?"

Chapter Twenty

"You have now joined the cause," Commander Stiessman's voice boomed from a loudspeaker fastened to a wall below a monitor in a large hall where three hundred enhanced and armed soldiers stood at attention in perfect rows. "And the cause is the noblest you will ever undertake—protecting the national security of Canada, destroying those who endeavor to harm us. By risking your lives, you will be offering the highest sacrifice, the most patriotic act one can make for the protection of homeland sovereignty. Please repeat after me. I swear my loyalty and allegiance to protecting Canada."

Nathan—first row, first in line—heard himself speak the words in perfect timing with the soldiers: "I swear my loyalty and allegiance to protecting Canada." But nothing registered. He was zombie-like, along with Velvet, standing right behind him, and along with the other 298 genetically modified soldiers. After being spotted in the deviant wing of District 101, the special building where the unenhanced military leaders brought "misbehaving" test subjects, Velvet and Nathan had been captured and tossed in lockdown in another facility near Stiessman's control tower. They had spent the night across the hall from one another in metal cubicles.

Captain Rice Sterling had notified Stiessman, who, after some consideration, had decided to release Velvet and Nathan, expose them to the warrior activation code for evaluation. Stiessman was under pressure from Prime Minister Masterson, who was cow-towing to pressure from US President Stintson to produce three hundred able-bodied and able-minded soldiers today. Stiessman didn't want to disappoint. His own agenda, his own master plan to have mountains of men under his sole command, was also at stake.

Through the monitor, Stiessman looked approvingly at his prodigies. The loudspeaker squawked with static before he resumed: "I swear to risk my life to unquestioningly fight for the safety of all citizens."

Like a well-trained boy-scout troupe, the soldiers repeated it.

"I will leave you to Captain Rice Sterling to explain the military exercise. Be brave, my soldiers. Be strong. Do I make myself clear?"

"Yes sir," the troops boomed, saluting.

Stiessman left.

To a hushed silence, Sterling entered the room, walked purposefully over to a podium with an attached microphone, and cleared his throat. It was the day he had waited all his life for, to have a platoon of soldiers, brave and loyal warriors who, under his command, would fight to the death for the cause. He scanned the hundreds of glazed, unfocused eyes and reflected on events leading up to this, his big moment.

His moment of total and complete control. Well, maybe not total control. But close enough for now. The rest, he knew, would come later.

It had started with his father Bryce telling Rice when he was six years old that "without control, you have nothing." He never forgot it. The axiom had been applied everywhere in Bryce's life, from his relationship with his timid wife Anise, who would grow quiet, her brow wrinkling slightly whenever Bryce exercised that control in his marriage, to the sub-contractors and employees he supervised in his mid-sized construction company in Toronto, Ontario. His father would not tolerate tardiness, sloppy personal hygiene, or his skewed definition of disrespect. Bryce's definition of the word was far-reaching. It could mean anything from joking around on a jobsite to shutting down and gathering tools two minutes before quitting time. During his years in elementary school, while on summer break, Rice would accompany his father to the office at least four times a week. Instead of playing with kids his age and doing what twelve-year-old boys do, he would sit at a small desk beside his father and learn "how to run a tight ship—with no disrespect."

As a child, Rice tried not to feel any sympathy for any of the employees he witnessed Bryce berate. But with Abe it was different. Abe Hanson was just different. A tall, geeky man with a mop of curly brown hair, everything Abe, a general laborer in the company, did seemed to piss off his father. From the laces on his steel-toed work boots being tied too loose, to a lock of his curly hair being out of place, Abe could do no right in Bryce's eyes. On one apartment building renovation, the ten employees were gathered in a small Atco trailer that served as a staff room next to another Atco trailer that was Bryce's office.

Rice would never forget that muggy Friday afternoon.

"Follow me, son," Bryce said, picking up a wad of paychecks and leaving the portable office. "I'll show you how to command respect." Rice got up from his little desk, where he was busy organizing the company's expenditures into neat little files, and followed.

Bryce stormed into the Atco trailer, where ten employees were waiting to get paid, changing to leave, grabbed Abe by the collar, and held a paycheck in front of his face. Abe's face turned bright red to a mix of grins, smiles and frowns. "This," Bryce said, "is your check. Let me ask you a question. Do you think you deserve it?"

Abe shrank back. "I've worked a full two weeks."

Bryce's face reddened and he tightened his grip on the shirt. "You call that work? You call leaving two-by-fours scattered on site while you go for a coffee break work? After I told you to clean them all up and make the site safe BEFORE you take coffee? You call coming in last Monday three minutes late work? You call heading to the Atco trailer at quarter to five work?"

"I had to go to the bathroom," Abe offered weakly.

Bryce ignored it. "All I get out of you is laziness and disrespect." He released the collar and pushed Abe forcefully into a locker. Abe lost his balance and almost fell on his ass, grabbing a locker handle at the last second and managing to stay on two feet.

A few employees laughed.

Bryce continued the reprimand, tearing Abe a brand-new asshole before almost tearing up his paycheck. "You don't deserve this," Bryce said, flicking Abe's cheek with the paycheck before flicking it into the air. It floated to the floor.

Abe bent down, picked up the check and moved toward the door, the sad and frightened look of a scolded schoolboy wrought into gaunt facial features.

"Get the hell out of here and don't ever come back," Bryce said as Abe closed the door. "I don't tolerate disrespect from my employees. Not now, not ever."

At a time when the economy wasn't that good, and jobs were hard to come by, it was all the other employees could do to meekly receive their paychecks and quietly leave.

Watching the public humiliation, Rice had turned his head toward a locker as he wiped away a lone tear. He knew to show weakness in front of Bryce would mean a severe private, perhaps even a public, reprimand. His existing asshole worked fine, thank you very much. He didn't want a new one. Not at twelve years old anyway.

When the last employee had left, Bryce turned to his son and said: "That's how you get respect, son. You'd be served well in your life to remember that."

As the scarring memory faded, Sterling inhaled deeply, searching the faces in the neat little rows. It was the only time he felt sorry for anyone his father had reprimanded and he wondered if Abe, that sorry assaulted soul, was anywhere in the room. After that, Sterling's life had been all about control. It didn't bother him that when he was fifteen years old his mother had disappeared one afternoon. She left a note, addressed to both Bryce and *my loving son*:

I'm tired of living in a house with control freaks. Don't you realize, control is an illusion? I'm leaving. Don't try and contact me. I probably won't contact you. I'm sorry, but it's either leave or end up in a loony bin. Rice, I'm sorry I didn't have the courage to make you a better man. I love you.

Bryce, you turned into a monster after we married. I used to love you. But it has long since been replaced by fear and loathing. Goodbye and good luck.

It was the last time he saw his mother. Two years later, he learned she had inserted a double-barreled shotgun into her mouth, pulled the trigger, and blown her brains out.

Maybe it was to try and hide all the pain. Maybe it was a competition to outdo his father in the control game. Sterling didn't know anymore, had long since given up wanting to know the reasons. On some level, maybe he thought he'd find them once he had total control of a platoon. He would put his late mother's theory to the test, about control being an illusion.

Oh no, he thought, turning away from unseeing eyes and wiping watery eyes. *This is no illusion. This is real. And it feels so good ... so good.* He turned to the soldiers, cleared his throat a second time, and began: "This is an exercise that will show you about discipline, respect and control. Do I have your attention?"

In unison: "YES SIR!"

"Good, let's go over the drill then ..."

******

Nathan and Velvet, in a squad with four other soldiers, crouched behind a rock outcrop about fifty feet from a wooden two-story house. There were enemies and civilians inside. It was their mission to kill the enemies and rescue all the civilians, or at least keep the collateral damage to a minimum. Velvet gave the command and Nathan and another soldier resembling GI Joe moved stealthily toward the target, ducking behind strategically placed rocks on route. A very real-looking little boy opened the front door and darted out. Nathan went to squeeze the trigger and stopped. GI Joe ran to the boy, swept him up in an arm and disappeared into a nearby bush. The barrel of a gun stuck out from a second-floor window and Nathan opened fire, felling the enemy with two shots to the head.

Another man, another window, another gun poked out. Velvet appeared behind Nathan, opening fire and riddling a line of six bullets in an upwardly curving line across the target's forehead.

"Uggghh," he said, not so mechanically, and fell through the window, shattering the glass and thudding onto the grass below.

Three team members scrambled to the rear of the house.

An AK-47-armed man leaped from the front door, spraying bullets. GI Joe reappeared, cut the enemy down with gunfire, and ran to the house, pressing himself tightly beside the front door. He waved Velvet and Nathan forward.

They sprinted to the house, pressing tightly into the wall behind GI Joe. Gunshots rang out from the second floor, more gunfire from behind the house.

"You," Velvet said, pointing to Nathan, then to the door.

"Me?" On some not quite coherent level of consciousness, he recognized, but not completely, the woman commanding him to smash through the door and lead the rescue operation. Then, the horrible nightmare he had been having almost every night up until a few days ago flashed through his mind; it had occurred so often, it hardly brought raw terror anymore, just an underlying below-the-surface kind of anticipatory dread; a dread that overlapped his perception of reality like the sticky silk of a black widow's deadly spider web. It was a pervading sensation of gloom and doom that overwhelmed his senses but yet he could not put a finger on it. That illogical and irrational feeling—often the precursor to a full-blown anxiety attack—that people say is nothing. "You're just being paranoid." And the certainty that accompanies it that they're wrong.

Dead wrong.

Nathan's arms stiffened. Abruptly he did feel it. Real fear. Raw fear. The kind that makes the hairs on the back of your neck stand up, the kind that makes you piss your pants, sweat, panic, kill, act and think in an illogical or logical way depending on how your fight-or-flight response is hardwired.

The nightmare flashed in his mind. A black hole. An unseen man, an ominous, powerful and dreadful presence. The voice—surreal yet eerily real at the same time. Ineffable. A voice of authority, wisdom and certainty. Dead certainty.

"Yes, you're going to die."

"When?"

"Very soon."

"How? How am I going to die?"

"Painfully."

But then another programmed and scientifically engineered voice quickly overrode it. *Complete the mission. Risk all for country. Die bravely and with honor.* And the scene looked familiar. This wasn't the first time he had been on this battlefield. No. The purple-black bruises on his knees, legs and arms. He had done this before. He knew what to do.

But Velvet wasn't taking any chances. She pointed the barrel of her AK-47 at his head. "Go."

More gunfire from above. GI Joe trained his assault rifle at the window and sprayed bullets. Another not-so-mechanical "ugghhh," another sack of hammers striking the ground with a thud.

Nathan stepped back and kicked the door hard, jumping aside as it flew open. Bullets sprayed out the entrance, some tearing into the wooden doorframe. The firing stopped. He ducked down and ran inside, his assault rifle lighting up a path of carnage as he shot the enemy. The fear was gone. The enemy were dead or dying. All that mattered was the mission.

More overhead fire. "I'm hit," GI Joe shouted, falling down, rolling and groaning.

Velvet glanced at the wounded soldier and a voice said, *Collateral damage ... complete the mission.* She stepped into the house and dove to the floor, firing as a hail of bullets blasted past.

Three soldiers entered from the rear. Bodies of the enemy were strewn on the floor. Five little children sat on the floor, wide-eyed, bound and gagged. A teary-eyed woman, zip-tied at the wrists and ankles, huddled beside them, offering words of comfort.

Getting to her feet, Velvet gave orders: "You two, check the main-floor rooms." Pointing to another soldier: "You, free the hostages." Then to Nathan: "Follow me upstairs."

To the sound of gunfire, they stealthily moved up the winding staircase. At the landing, Velvet said, "Take that room. I'll be in the hall."

Nathan didn't waste any time. He kicked open the door and rushed inside, immediately spotting Melvin Tierney, armed, standing over three zip-tied children huddled together cross-legged on the floor.

Do I know him? Nathan thought. But another voice in his head spoke louder and clearer as a tiny red dot danced on Melvin's forehead: *The enemy. Kill the enemy. Save the children.*

Melvin, sweat dripping down his face, hands shaking, reached for a pistol holstered around his waist. "It's one big fucking melting pot," he said. "And you know what?"

Nathan massaged the trigger, the red dot now steady between Melvin's eyes. *Kill the enemy. Save the children.*

"We're all fucking melting together," Melvin said, drawing his handgun.

Nathan didn't know why, but he aimed slightly left and riddled the wall behind Melvin with bullets as the children covered ears with hands and screamed.

Melvin inserted the gun barrel into his mouth, grinned maniacally, and pulled the trigger. *Kaplow!* Blood and brain matter splattered the window behind him, a tie-dyed mosaic of red and gray. He slumped to the floor. A screaming child crawled swiftly out of the way to avoid getting squashed.

From down the hall, Nathan heard Velvet's voice: "Back-up. I need back-up."

As another soldier entered and began freeing grateful but traumatized children, Nathan ran down the hall to where Velvet stood outside a closed door riddled with bullet holes, a strange voice echoing dimly from inside.

She gave the command and Nathan booted it open, entering with his rifle trained on Doctor Stan Imes, who was standing beside a window, blood dripping from a bullet wound to his right bicep. Nathan didn't hesitate, steadying a twirling red dot on Imes's forehead. He was just about to pull the trigger when Imes said: "B4632106."

Nathan lowered the machine gun, glancing around the room in disbelief. "What's going on?" he said, noticing Velvet had lowered her weapon and was staring at Imes in disbelief.

"Violence deactivation code," Imes said. "You're a genetically modified warrior."

"What?" Nathan asked.

"I knew it," Velvet said. Turning to Nathan: "What have I been saying all along? Anti-radiation pills my ass. They're turning us into killing machines."

"You've got to get me out of here," Imes said, holding his bleeding bicep, blood spurting between his fingers and dripping down his arm. He was unarmed.

Velvet trained her weapon on Imes's head. "What? Get you outta here? You gotta be nuts. You've been in on this all along."

"I was, but not anymore," Imes pleaded. "Sterling, Laines, Stiessman—they're all nuts. Serious problems with P-744 and they're ignoring them. They want me dead ... wanted you to kill me."

Flashbacks of the macabre scene in the deviant wing clicked through Nathan's mind. "He's right, let's get him out of here."

"Not so fast," Velvet said, as two soldiers appeared at the door. A lingering memory of her authority remained. "Situation contained," she said, waving them out. "We'll rendezvous outside in two minutes."

The soldiers retreated downstairs as she slammed shut what remained of the door and swung around to Imes.

A siren wailed in the distance, slowly growing louder and echoing eerily in the dome.

"What makes you think we can trust you?" she said, stepping toward Imes. "Let's waste him."

"I know how to escape," Imes said.

"To where?" Nathan asked, violent images of battles with the savage Neanderthals flashing through his mind.

"We'll go to Prince Edward Island," Imes said. "Start anew."

"You've got to be kidding me," Velvet said. "After the shit-storm we suffered there?"

"Listen," Imes said. "We're running out of time. Sterling will be here any minute. And he'll take us all out."

Nathan extracted a handgun from his shoulder holster and offered it to Imes. "Take it. You're gonna need it."

Velvet stepped forward, grabbing the handgun. "Not so fast. We can't trust this fucker any more than we can trust anyone else here. He's behind this nightmare."

They wrestled for control of the piece while Imes watched, beady eyes wide with terror.

Velvet elbowed Nathan in the stomach. Winded, he released the piece, took a knee, and started coughing.

Footfalls ascending stairs thumped, growing nearer.

Catching his breath, Nathan pleaded. "Please, Velvet. It's not like we have a lot of options."

She leveled the handgun at Imes's head.

Imes froze.

She cocked the hammer, massaged the trigger.

"Come on," Nathan said, still on one knee. "Let's get out of here."

"Sterling will kill us all," Imes said. "You kill me, you're both dead."

The footfalls clocked purposefully down the hall toward them.

Velvet lowered the weapon and stepped toward Imes. "You so much as think about harming us and you'll get a bullet bloodbath." She moved to within a few inches from his face. "You got that?"

Imes, jittering, nodded.

She handed Imes the gun.

He took it.

The footfalls stopped outside the door. Nathan and Velvet swung around, riddling it with bullets. It flung off its hinges and landed on two dead soldiers. Nathan stepped out into the hallway and gunned down a third soldier who was moving toward them in the hallway. The soldier moaned and dropped dead.

Nathan stood guard in the hall. It grew quiet, the echo of gunfire subsiding.

Inside the room, Imes tore a strip from his shirtsleeve and fashioned a tourniquet. He wrapped it tightly around his injured bicep. "It's just a graze. No bullet inside."

The roar of an incoming vehicle engine sounded. Nathan went inside the room and looked out the window. A green army jeep pulled in front of the house, stopped abruptly, and two soldiers got out, waving and uttering commands to the team huddled outside. Having completed their mission, some assault team members stood purposeless next to a group of rescued children and adults. But the commands turned heads to the second-floor window. A soldier raised an assault rifle to fire. Nathan sprayed him with bullets before he could press the trigger, and he dropped. "Get down," Nathan yelled. "We got incoming."

They dove to the floor as a barrage of machine-gun fire assaulted the building, bullets tearing into the wooden exterior, smashing through the window, sending glass scimitars flying, bullets whizzing and ricocheting around the room. Nathan and Velvet opened fire, hearing at least one moan in the melee, and saw a man fall to the ground. Nathan poked his head out again and saw it—a rocket launcher pointed at the window. "Get the hell out," he shouted. "Bomb incoming!"

They cleared the room, diving into the hallway as the bomb exploded the small bedroom with a thunderous boom and a whooshing ball of flame, raining debris on three prostrate bodies. Velvet was the first to move, shaking off the shellshock and debris, slowly standing. "Downstairs. Now," she said, leading the way as two men rushed through the front door, pointed automatic weapons in the stairwell, and opened fire. Velvet and Nathan sprayed bullets at the attackers, cutting them down.

Doctor Imes, wide-eyed, held his handgun with a trembling hand, unable to pull the trigger.

"You better know how to use that," Velvet said as they huddled in what was left of an adjoining upper-floor room.

"I know how to use it. We're all trained in weapons handling. But I've never had to shoot anybody."

"But it's all right for you to fuck with their heads and turn them—turn us—into killing machines," Velvet said, before resuming fire.

Nathan poked his gun out and cut down two more attacking soldiers before he saw another man loading up a rocket launcher. "Fuck, it's time."

They descended the stairs and reached the main floor. Nathan glanced quickly around. Incoming soldiers everywhere. It was now or never. He bolted out the front door, scrambling for the jeep while firing. He killed two men before arriving, and climbed in. The engine was still running.

Velvet, meanwhile, crouched down behind a rock outcrop just outside the house and began shooting at soldiers from other assault teams who were moving across the grass toward them.

Two more jeeps barreled up the road toward them.

Nathan drove to the house entrance and waved them in. Velvet climbed in the front passenger seat while Imes got in the back seat. Just as Nathan accelerated, an incoming missile impacted the house, blowing it up with a large boom. A ball of flame engulfed the house, exploding into the air, twirling black spiraling smoke up to the sky. Debris rained everywhere.

Nathan sped out of the training compound, tailed now by two jeeps and an armored personnel carrier. A rocket launcher hung out the window of a jeep that was rapidly closing the distance.

"Incoming," Imes said.

"First decent thing I've seen you do," Velvet said as Nathan jerked the jeep hard right. The bomb exploded a few feet left, rocketing rear wheels airborne. They hit the road hard, the jeep fishtailing erratically before Nathan finally brought it under control and put pedal to metal.

"Where to?" he asked.

"The deviant complex," Imes said.

"Deviant complex?" Velvet said as bullets whizzed past the speeding jeep.

"Someone shoot, for fuck sakes," Nathan said.

"You fucking scumbags," Imes shouted, swinging around and opening fire. A bullet punctured a front tire of the closest pursuing jeep and it spun out of control and flipped end-over-end twice before crash-landing on its hood and exploding with a deafening boom.

"Second decent thing," Velvet said.

"Which road?" Nathan asked. They were barreling down a two-lane gravel road surrounded by woods. A sliver of orange sun was visible in the distance as it crested the tree line. The rest of the sky was ominously gray-black.

"Second sharp right turn," Velvet said. "I know where it is."

"That's right," Imes agreed, punctuating his words with two gunshots aimed at the pursuers. One shot penetrated a windshield and the jeep behind them spun out of control, veered off the road, hit the ditch and launched into the air. It flew fifty feet or so before landing on its hood, scraping metal, bursting into flames, and exploding.

"Three times lucky," Velvet offered.

"I'm out of bullets," Imes said.

Velvet handed him a clip, stood up in the jeep, and began spraying bullets at the armored vehicle.

"That won't penetrate an armored car," Imes said, picking up a rocket launcher that had been left in the jeep. He pointed to a metal box on the floor. "There are missiles in there," he said, snapping the chamber open. "Load me up."

"Four times and I'm going to kiss you," Velvet said, opening the box and jamming a rocket in the chamber. He closed it, aimed, and pulled the trigger. The missile struck the ground in front of the vehicle. It veered around it, careening dangerously close to the ditch before slowing, stabilizing, and resuming chase.

"At least I bought us some time," Imes said.

"Not worth a kiss," Velvet said with a tone of mock petulance. *Is this the P-744 talking? What the fuck's gotten into me?* Then, to Nathan: "Your next hard right."

He slowed and fishtailed the jeep into the corner, spinning tires on loose gravel before finding traction and continuing down the road toward the deviant complex.

Velvet glanced back. "We're running out of time. Step on it!"

"The complex is fully guarded," Imes said. "Our only chance is to crash the left wing door, where the deviants are held. Free them."

"Take the dirt road before the entrance," Velvet said. "They'll be expecting us at the main entrance."

She pointed ahead and Nathan saw it—the same road they had taken when they stole the electric vehicle and bore witness to the macabre goings-on inside the wing. He spun the jeep into the corner, slowed while continuing down its windy and bumpy path, careened around another corner that lead to the small hole in the fence, and stopped.

They stared at the fence in the distance, topped with barbed wire. Shots rang out from the watchtower, a siren wailed, and men inside the compound mobilized. The small hole they had climbed through earlier had been repaired.

Nathan looked questioningly at Imes, then at Velvet. "You guys ready?"

"Crash it," Velvet said.

"Go for it," Imes said.

"Duck down," Nathan said, applying the brake, revving the motor for a few seconds before popping the brake. The jeep spun dirt before the off-road tires gripped, lurching forward, barreling toward the fence. As they approached, Velvet raised her machine gun, spraying it with bullets. She punctured a small opening in the fence and the jeep crashed into it, tearing through the metal and into the compound.

"There," Imes pointed as gunfire erupted. "Crash into that door."

As bullets zinged past, Nathan gunned it toward the door, towing a chunk of metal fence that had snagged on the rear differential. "Everybody down," he shouted as the vehicle impacted steel and concrete. It stopped halfway inside, rear tires spinning on chunks of broken concrete and steel as the motor revved. Nathan wiped away concrete dust from his eyes, taking stock of his passengers. Velvet had a cut on her forehead and was slumped face-first into the windshield, unconscious.

Imes stuck his head out from a pile of debris and climbed out.

Nathan shook Velvet. "Wake up. Velvet, wake up."

Her eyes slowly opened. They rolled around in her head. Blood from the two-inch gash on her forehead poured down her nose and into her eyes. Nathan wiped her face with a hand. "We've got to go."

To shouts, cackles and taunts, Imes went into a hallway surrounded by incarcerated test subjects. He hurried down the hall and entered a room. He closed the door behind him, found an access panel, and punched in his password. A series of buzzers sounded and cell doors in the entire wing clanged open. Deviants flooded into the hallways, some climbing over the jeep and fleeing from their incarceration.

As sirens wailed, gunfire erupted, and inmates escaped, Nathan pulled Velvet from the jeep and followed the escaping masses outside the complex. It was complete pandemonium as soldiers approached, momentarily distracted from their pursuit of Velvet, Nathan and Imes, and began shooting crazed inmates.

Imes appeared outside and pointed to a black circular manhole cover. "In there."

Nathan shot an approaching guard in the head and then froze in his tracks. A black mass of clouds descended on the man-made habitat. Thunder boomed and lightning popped and sizzled. A lightning bolt snaked down from the sky and struck the dome. It popped loudly and fizzled. A tiny crack appeared and morphed into a rapidly growing spider web of cracks. He looked to the ocean and his heart almost leaped from his chest. A giant wall of water, at least three hundred feet high, thrust forward with deadly speed.

The guards and the fleeing deviants all saw it too. Some stopped and stared, frozen in terror.

Imes broke Nathan and Velvet from their mesmerized stupor. "The shaft ... let's go."

A gigantic wave crashed into the cracked dome and it shattered. A torrent of powerfully flowing water raced toward them, felling trees, decimating buildings, washing away panicked humans, sweeping automobiles like tin cans along its violent swath of destruction. An even bigger wave, maybe a hundred feet away, was closing fast.

They reached the black manhole-like cover as people screamed, panicked, and ran for their lives. Imes, Velvet and Nathan cranked the wheel together. It opened. Velvet climbed in and Imes followed while Nathan struggled with a panicking deviant escapee who had tackled him and was sitting on his chest, pinning him.

"Let me go," Nathan shouted. "The shaft. I'll take you with us."

The danger wasn't registering on the bearded man's face. His black eyes were glazed over. He grinned at Nathan. "I'm going to fuck you up the ass."

Nathan grunted and squirmed but was no match for the man's weight. "Get off me. We're going to die," he said, pointing to the approaching wave carrying screaming, drowning people and all manner of debris.

Velvet poked her machine gun from the hole and shot the man in the face. "You ain't fucking anyone up the ass." Blood sprayed from his face, showering Nathan with red droplets. The man slumped over. Nathan grunted and twisted free.

Velvet extended a hand and Nathan grabbed it, just as water began lashing at his legs, threatening to wash him away with the other victims. By now, water was also rushing into the small shaft.

"Hurry," Velvet said.

With a final effort, he crawled forward, pulling on Velvet's outstretched arm until he reached the hole. Imes grabbed Nathan's free hand. Bombarded by cascading water, they yanked him inside.

"Give me a hand," Velvet shouted, trying to close the steel lid while water gushed in. Imes helped while Nathan clung to a steel ladder wrung, coughing and spewing seawater mixed with dirt and debris. A dead body smashed into the manhole cover door, slamming it shut as a blast of water exploded in, dislodging Nathan and Imes and sweeping them down the shaft in a violent wash. Velvet clung to the inside of the door and finally managed to twist it shut before another powerful blast of water poured in from an exploding inside airshaft and sent her spiraling down the winding shaft in a powerful jet.

Further down the shaft, Nathan coughed, spewed water, and clung on for dear life. After a rapid, winding downward thrust—he could just make out Imes's head and hand protruding in front of him as they blasted along—they ended up on top of a level steel bridge, three manhole covers marking its path into more metal tunnels. Nathan's arm was wrapped around a steel wheel, a door handle of sorts to another tunnel or network of tunnels. He watched the water recede, knowing it wouldn't be long before more gushed in, perhaps obliterating District 101.

Imes clung to a steel handle mounted on the wall of the rectangular-shaped small bridge. He was coughing violently.

"You okay?" Nathan asked.

Imes nodded, but continued coughing and spitting water.

"Velvet? Where's Velvet?" Nathan asked.

Imes stopped coughing and pointed. Her body crunched beside a circular opening that emptied into the larger opening where they were. Nathan coughed and expelled seawater. When he was able to breathe better, he staggered over to her. "Velvet? Are you okay?"

She didn't answer. Her eyes were lifeless, her face expressionless. Nathan held a hand to her neck. No pulse. "Imes," he shouted. "Give me a hand here."

Nathan tugged Velvet's leg, trying to free her from the crevice.

Imes struggled to his feet and approached. After some wrenching and a few cuss words they pulled her free, positioning her on her back. Suffused gray light cast a deathly glow on her face.

"She's not breathing," Nathan shouted. "For fuck sakes, do something."

The underground structure began creaking and groaning metallically and an eerie whooshing sound started, soft at first, but it grew steadily louder, the angry hiss of an attacking serpent of liquid death.

Imes pointed to a black manhole cover. "Open that." He began mouth-to-mouth resuscitation on Velvet.

Imes held her nose and breathed in her lungs for a minute or so. "Shit, she's not responding." The creaks and groans intensified. "We're running out of time."

"Keep going," Nathan said, struggling to open the steel lid. It creaked and slowly started turning. "I'm not leaving without her."

Imes breathed into Velvet's lungs again. Her body suddenly twitched and she spewed a fountain of water that splashed off Imes's face. She began coughing and spitting water. Imes lifted her to a sitting position, pounded on her back, and tilted her head forward as more water poured from her mouth. When she stopped vomiting and caught her breath, she asked, "Did you give me mouth-to-mouth?"

Imes nodded.

"There," she said, trying unsuccessfully to stand and flopping into the wall as Imes steadied her with a hand. She kissed him on the cheek. "That's the kiss I promised you."

"Along with a little saltwater bath," he said.

She smiled weakly. "Better that than the kiss of death." But listening to the cascading water growing louder, the smile quickly turned into a frown.

Nathan opened the manhole lid. The water was coming like rolling thunder now. A nearby manhole cover exploded, water frothing out, its lid clanging off steel tunnel walls as it bounced around forcefully.

"Get in here. Both of you!" Nathan said.

"Where does it go?" Velvet asked, climbing in.

"It's a submarine base below here," Imes said.

The last one in, Nathan closed the lid as water gushed in. They clung to metal ladder rungs until the cascading water stopped soaking them. Nathan looked down. The descending tunnel was lit every ten feet with small gray light bulbs protected by small round metal cages. A back-up generator must have kicked in, he thought, grimly realizing District 101 was already underwater permanently. A backlash by Mother Nature? Or maybe the North Koreans, who, according to Stiessman, had dropped the initial nuclear bomb. Maybe they had decided to finish the job they started and drop another bomb in the ocean to create the giant swell of death? *Maybe I'll never get the answers.*

They could hear water rushing as the small chamber above began filling up. It was rapidly becoming a death chamber.

They began their descent, Imes leading, Velvet in the middle, and Nathan following.

"You know how to run a submarine, Imes?" Nathan asked as they progressed. His voice echoed hollowly in the confined quarters.

"Yes. When I was first recruited, I had special passage to District 101, to the deviant wing. That sub below practically runs itself."

"Imes, I think you better learn something about terminology," Velvet said. "Those people who are likely all dead now aren't deviants. They were normal people until you and the government started fucking with their heads. Why did they react the way they did, anyway?"

"It has to do with blood type," Imes explained. "They're blood type A. We don't know why, but that blood type creates some rather deviant sexual behavior. The plan was to create a population that was free on one hand, under complete government control on the other—when it came to defending our country. Things got a little out of hand, I'm afraid. They wanted to replace me, tried to kill me. I wasn't getting the results they wanted fast enough. And too many people with their own agendas."

"A little out of hand?" Velvet said with rising agitation. "People having sudden urges to kill people and fuck people to death, and that's 'a little out of hand'? It's not only blood type A, either. How do you explain my urges? I wanted to kill Nathan a few times? Maybe even fuck him to death." She made a disgusted face. "And I actually kissed you earlier."

"I thought about killing you," Nathan admitted to Velvet. "I thought it was my own fucked up psyche."

"Oh, your psyche is fucked up," Velvet said.

"Tell me about it."

"You walked right into it."

Nathan envisaged a marathon fuck-fest with Velvet, each one trying to outperform the other until one of them was no longer breathing—fucked to death. Not a bad way to go, he thought, considering the alternatives in this so-called new world order, a world where if you weren't afraid of yourself, it was your neighbor or best friend you had to fear. And if that wasn't enough, there was the government itself, trying to enhance you, make you into the perfect, law-abiding citizen one moment, the perfect warrior the next. An unquestioning and devoted soldier who would—at the utterance of a code word—drop everything for "the cause" and be willing to mercilessly kill for reasons that would probably never be made clear. *The cause? Where did I come up with that?* Then an image of Rice Sterling flashed into Nathan's mind. He was starting to remember some things he wasn't supposed to. All this time, he had been reluctant to believe Velvet. He'd thought it had something to do with his amnesia-producing accident, the loss of his soulmate Cadence, or all the ugly shit he had suffered and survived with the zombies, the mutant animals, The Neanderthals, all coming back to haunt him.

The Neanderthals. The zombies. The mutant animals. *Wait a minute. We're going back to that shit-storm.* He stopped, pulled a hand off a steel wrung, and clenched his fist, waving it into the air angrily as he heard the footfalls of Imes and Velvet making time ahead. He could hear a faint sound of water swishing below, perhaps fifty feet or so. "Wait a fucking minute," Nathan said.

The footfalls stopped.

"What?" Imes said.

"You oversaw this project. You fucked with our heads. Now, through no fault of my own, I have these urges to kill Velvet. How do I know the urges won't transfer to others? How do I know I won't act them out? How the fuck do I know anything now that you've fucked with my already fucked up psyche? You oughta be ashamed of yourself, Doctor Imes—oughta be ashamed to call yourself a doctor."

Imes said, "Listen ... I had no idea things would get this bad. I thought I could perfect the drug, do something noble and beneficial for humankind. I guess it didn't turn out that way ... I *am* ashamed of myself ... and I'm sorry, for what it's worth."

"You still didn't answer the question," Velvet said.

"I didn't know there was a question," Imes said.

"What about us?" Velvet said. "What's going to happen to us now ... now that we're not taking P-744?"

"I have an underground lab in PEI," Imes said. "If we can get there, I think I can reverse the effects ... at least minimize them to a manageable level."

Nathan still had his fist clenched. "Manageable level?" he snapped. "You mean we're stuck with these urges for the rest of our lives?"

"I have some experimental drugs," Imes said. "I should be able to help. Let me try. Please."

"What fucking choice do we have?" Velvet said.

"Do we have any guarantees we won't fly off the handle?" Nathan asked.

"I'm sorry," Imes said. "I'm afraid not."

Chapter Twenty-One

Nathan wasn't afraid when they reached the submarine launch pad at the bottom of the tunnel and two soldiers pointed assault rifles at his head. He was a soldier following orders, completing a mission. He and Velvet had, albeit reluctantly, agreed to let Imes utter the violence-activation code. So, now they were in warrior mode, with Imes, their new commander, calling the shots. And fear wasn't a part of that chemical programming.

Imes decided to try the diplomatic tact first. "I'm Doctor Imes," he told the soldiers. "Lower your weapons. We have a disaster on our hands and the first priority is the safety of our civilians."

Nathan reached for a holstered handgun and took one step toward the soldiers.

"Put another finger on that gun and I blow your brains out," the soldier said.

Velvet quickly drew her handgun and leveled it at the soldier's head.

"And the same goes for your bitch," the soldier said. "Tell her to lower that fucking weapon."

"Zero-seven, lower your weapon," Imes said. "Zero-eight, don't take the bait."

Velvet lowered her handgun while Nathan slid a hand away from his holstered weapon. They both stared at Imes blankly, awaiting their orders.

Imes pointed to a small black submarine floating in an oval-shaped pool surrounded by jagged rocks. A steel platform jutted out at one corner, extending about six feet into the watery opening.

District 101 rumbled, groaned and started shaking violently. Large waves washed over the submarine.

The soldiers stepped back to avoid getting splashed or falling in.

Nathan drew his gun and fired two bullets, one piercing his eye, the other smashing through his skull just above the eye.

Velvet shot the other soldier once in the head and twice in the heart. He sprayed a short burst of machine gun fire as he was falling.

Imes, Velvet and Nathan dove for cover as bullets whizzed everywhere.

"Zero-seven, zero-eight ... I told you not to fire."

"Collateral damage, commander," they said in unison. "Our loyalty is to our nation, sir."

The ground trembled vigorously and the cave began cracking. Steel creaked and groaned overhead. "Into the sub," Imes ordered. "Now!"

He walked briskly to the violently shaking steel bridge. He inched his way out to the rocking submarine, slipped and started falling. Nathan grabbed his arm and steadied him. "You want to be careful, sir."

They reached the submarine and Nathan pulled open the top hatch. He stood aside while Velvet and Imes entered.

Debris rained everywhere and water began pouring in from cracks in the ceiling. Nathan quickly climbed in and closed the hatch just as a large metal ceiling beam unhinged and crashed onto the submarine, clanging loudly and shaking it forcefully.

When it steadied, they descended a steel ladder into a control room. Imes fiddled with a few controls. The submarine whirred to life and plunged underwater just as a huge boulder came crashing down, narrowly missing it.

******

"B4632106," Imes said.

Nathan looked around in bewilderment at the control room. So did Velvet.

Imes sat on a padded steel chair bolted to the floor. He stared at a computer radar screen.

"Is the mission over?" Nathan asked.

"What mission?" Velvet said.

"The mission's over," Imes said, pressing a few buttons and scanning the computer monitors. Through a circular, thick glass window on a wall above the controls, they could barely see where they were going. The ocean was black.

A large boulder clanged off the submarine, the deafening, tinny sound echoing through its small metal chamber. The submarine rocked back and forth for a few seconds. Nathan, Velvet and Imes grabbed steel handles welded on walls and steadied themselves. Soon, Imes righted the vessel and a smooth descent commenced.

But a loud overhead explosion rocked the tiny submarine so powerfully Velvet and Nathan slammed into a wall while Imes clung to a metal rail with both hands.

Finally, he righted the craft by pressing a series of buttons and the descent continued, the explosions becoming less ferocious and less frequent.

Nathan and Velvet picked themselves up, moved toward the steel handles beside Imes, and clung on with both hands as the submarine whirred into the ocean depths with a renewed precision and quiet.

Nathan released one hand from the handle and relaxed slightly. He watched Velvet follow suit. Then he got a first-aid kit and, following Imes's instructions, bandaged Velvet's head wound.

She didn't protest.

"It's okay now," Imes said. "I think we're out of the worst of it."

"The worst of it may be yet to come," Nathan said.

Imes stared at them in silence, stone-faced and somber.

Velvet touched the head gauze, winced slightly, and nodded.

******

Curled up an hour later in a tiny bunk in his private sleeping quarters, Nathan's mind swam. District 101 undoubtedly was completely destroyed by the tsunami wave, and it was anyone's guess how many others had escaped. Somehow, he thought Sterling and Stiessman were among that mix. His gut said they had anticipated, if not caused, the destruction of District 101.

Worrying about how he would ever survive, how he could keep on going in the face of so much adversity, Nathan tossed and turned on the small cot. After a fitful hour, a thin disturbed sleep finally enveloped his consciousness. And the nightmare of old returned, more menacing and frightening than before.

He was in a dark tunnel, plodding along, a crude loincloth his only protection from the cold. Wind howled from somewhere high above, and his feet shivered as they touched the cold, rocky surface. He stopped and rubbed his hands together, blowing warm breath into them. He briskly rubbed his chest and arms, shivered, and continued. *Gotta make a fire ... gotta make fire.* He rounded a corner and came to an opening not unlike the opening he had first found himself in when he had met his protector, the late Edward Sole, the man whose spirit continued to haunt his waking and sleeping hours.

He sat down cross-legged, hugged himself for warmth for a while, and then noticed it—a pile of twigs and some matches. He quickly snapped off a few twigs and placed them in a round circle of rocks. *What?* he thought, horrified. The rocks were exactly the same size and shape—the same crooked formation, even—as the fire pit in the network of tunnels where he had struggled to survive. His heart began thumping wildly in his chest and lighting the fire was all he could do to prevent himself from screaming bloody murder. *Hang on. Get yourself warm.*

Soon, he had a respectable fire going and was beginning to warm up, the heat going some way to relieve cold terror. *Maybe I'll be okay?* He tried a smile that was quickly interrupted by a voice.

"You're going to die."

The voice was familiar. Edward Sole. "Ed? Is that you?"

Out of the blackness, a man appeared. As he approached the fire and regarded Nathan, his features came into focus. Head shaved, skinny chest riddled with bullets that oozed blood. Black war paint streaked across chest. More black war paint on his gaunt and war-worn face. Beady eyes that blazed red. The same crooked, not quite sane, smile. "I tried to warn you before," Ed said slowly. "You're finally starting to remember. All this time ..."

"That was you before. Tell me now ... who's going to kill me."

"In time, young son. In time. You're not ready."

"Ed, for fuck sakes, I'm as ready as I'll ever be. Tell me! Please, tell me!"

"Learn to embrace it. For it will be an end to misery ... an end to a world of pain and suffering."

"Okay ... okay, I'll embrace it. Just tell me. Who's going to kill me?"

There was a long silence, punctuated by the crackling and popping of the fire, the ferocious wind howling overhead.

Nathan realized grimly he had returned to where the entire nightmare had started.

Ed turned and walked away, his misty gray image fading into blackness.

"No, Ed, don't go. Tell me who!"

And as the apparition was enveloped in blackness, three words echoed hollowly in the dark cave: "Captain Rice Sterling."

Chapter Twenty-Two

Sterling admired Commander Stiessman as he expertly navigated the military chopper over the giant tsunami wave that washed over District 101, completely obliterating it. *A hands-on commander. I like that.*

A series of loud explosions punctuated the crushing wave, but by then the chopper was well out of danger and didn't even receive any aftershocks from the blasts. Jeffery Laines sat beside Stiessman while Sterling paced restlessly behind them.

Sterling glared at the red blip on the radar screen and waited until the booming from two military jets passing overhead faded before speaking. "There it is sir," he said, pointing to the screen. "That's Imes, zero-seven and zero-eight. They killed another two of our own before boarding. We have a sub a mile and a half northwest of them, within striking distance. Should I give the order to fire?"

"No, Sterling," Stiessman said impatiently, returning to the chopper controls. "I told you. I want to monitor their progress on PEI before we take any action. You know they'll be forced to fight savage Neanderthals. That's what we trained them for. I want to see how they do."

"But, sir, we have other trained soldiers—"

"What other trained soldiers?" Stiessman snapped. "Most of them are dead. We have ... what, twenty-two survivors?"

"Twenty-three who are ready to go to war."

Stiessman's eyes narrowed as he navigated the chopper through a mass of gray-black clouds. "We've lost over eleven thousand enhanced soldiers in that fucking natural disaster—which I'm still not convinced was completely natural, by the way—and you want to send our only twenty-two survivors into PEI now? Captain, you're not thinking. First we need to work out the kinks from P-744. In the meantime, I want those twenty-two—twenty-three—survivors locked down on the first aircraft carrier we can find that hasn't been destroyed by that fucking tidal wave. Sterling, I wish you would use your God-given brain for once in your life."

Stiessman returned his attention to the chopper's controls.

Sterling extracted a handgun, pressed it to the side of Stiessman's head, and pulled the trigger. A loud blast echoed deafeningly through the small cockpit, and a gray-red mash splattered onto controls, metal and glass.

"With all due respect, that's what I'm doing, sir," Sterling said. "Using my brain."

Stiessman slumped over and the chopper jerked violently, starting a rapid, spinning nosedive.

Sterling grabbed Stiessman's medal-studded jacket collar, yanked him roughly out of the cockpit, and glared into Jeffery Laines's horrified eyes. "Don't just fucking gawk at me, numb-nuts. Take the controls."

Nervously Laines climbed into the pilot seat and steadied the out-of-control chopper. Sterling dragged Stiessman's body to a side door, slid it open, and tossed the former commander into the ocean. Then he walked casually over to the radar, picked up a two-way radio, pressed a button, and spoke. "Black Dog, this is Blue Tornado, do you read?"

"Roger that, Blue Tornado."

"Black Dog, you're green on target Imes."

"Roger that, Blue Tornado. Go on green. Over and out."

The End

Also by William Blackwell

Phantom Rage, Poison Rage, Infected Rage
Nightmare's Edge
Resurrection Point
Brainstorm
Rule 14
Assaulted Souls
Assaulted Souls II
Assaulted Souls III
Blood Curse
Black Dawn
The Strap
The End is Nigh
Orgon Conclusion
Freaky Franky
The Witch's Tombstone
The Dark Menace
Tales of Damnation
In Your Dreams
Macabre Alley
A Head for an Eye

Assaulted Souls III Preview

"This novel is as action-packed as the others but it is this final book where I personally felt I was really connecting to the characters." -For the Novel Lovers blog

What if the government made it mandatory for you to have a microchip implanted in your brain, saying it was for your security? Would you believe it? Would you take it?

What if you learned world powers were setting up sophisticated spy cameras everywhere to watch and record your every move 24/7? Would you believe it? Would you run and hide? Would you become a subversive and fight back?

What if you learned soldiers and law-enforcement officers had become super soldiers, genetically modified trans-humans capable of outrunning Usain Bolt, out-lifting Olympic weightlifters, re-growing limbs, and even communicating telepathically through microchips installed in their brains? Would you believe it? Would you acquiesce? Would you revolt?

In a chillingly real examination of these questions, post-apocalyptic disaster survivors Nathan King and Velvet Jones escape government clutches, returning to war-ravaged Prince Edward Island only to discover a living nightmare. They are thrust into a fierce battle with savage, opportunistic tribes struggling for survival; demented military soldiers, and giant insects created by the new world order.

"William Blackwell delivers in this post-apocalyptic thriller. Couldn't put it down." -Amazon

About the Author

Canadian dark fiction author William Blackwell studied journalism at Mount Royal University and English literature at The University of British Columbia. He worked as a journalist and a newspaper editor for many years before pursuing his passion for storytelling. His novels have been characterized as graphic, edgy, and at times terrifying. Currently living on a secluded acreage on Prince Edward Island, Blackwell finds much of his inspiration from Mother Nature, odd people, traveling, and bizarre nightmares.

Author Comments

Thank you for reading this book. I would be eternally grateful if you would post a book review on your favorite book retailer website. A positive review is the highest compliment a writer can receive. Reviews are crucial to the success of any author and also help readers discover books. You don't have to say much. A few sentences will suffice.

In other news, I have a gift for you. Complete the signup form below with your name and email address and download a FREE copy of *Resurrection Point*, a dark tale about the horrifying consequences of experimenting with death and resurrection. You're only agreeing to be kept up to date on blog posts, new releases, and freebies. I promise I won't spam you and you can unsubscribe at any time.

Thanks again for your support.

http://www.wblackwell.com/free-ebook/

www.ingramcontent.com/pod-product-compliance
Lightning Source LLC
Chambersburg PA
CBHW021010180626
46814CB00003B/1228